Lily lay on the bed, feeling Charlotte's gaze burn through her. In everyday life, Lily felt she was passably attractive in a sloppy, bohemian kind of way, but she certainly wasn't the kind of person who turned heads — male or female.

In the world of their bedroom, though, Charlotte made Lily feel like a high-femme fantasy figure. In Charlotte's eyes, in Charlotte's hands, she was Rita Hayworth . . . Marilyn Monroe.

When Charlotte finally joined Lily on the bed, their lips met in a fierce, bruising kiss. Lily wrapped her arms and legs around her lover, who pressed down on her, as each of them tried to get as close to the other as possible.

Charlotte pulled down the shoulder strap of Lily's black dress and kissed her from shoulder to collarbone to breast. And when Charlotte's hand slipped between Lily's legs . . .

LOOKING FOR NAIAD?

Buy our books at
www.naiadpress.com

or call our toll-free number
1-800-533-1973

or by fax (24 hours a day)
1-850-539-9731

Wedding Bell Blues

JULIA WATTS

THE NAIAD PRESS, INC.
1999

Printed in the United States of America on acid-free paper
First Edition

Editor: Lila Empson
Cover designer: Bonnie Liss (Phoenix Graphics)
Typesetter: Sandi Stancil

Library of Congress Cataloging-in-Publication Data

Watts, Julia, 1969 –
    Wedding bell blues / by Julia Watts.
        p.   cm.
    ISBN 1-56280-230-5   (alk. paper)
    I. Title.
PS3573.A868W4   1999
813'.54—dc21   98-44750
                                                                              CIP

Acknowledgments

According to popular myth, writers are solitary folk who take long, lonely walks or stare at blank walls for hours on end, waiting for inspiration to strike. I do not work this way. In order to be productive, I must be surrounded by fellow writers, family members, and long-suffering friends who are willing to listen to me babble excitedly about my current project when it's going well . . . and to me whine about when it's going slowly. Thanks to all of you who have given me support in person, in letters, or in e-mail: Carol, Don, Ian, Mom, Dad, Jim, Dwane, Allison, Stephanie, Tab, Keri, Helen, Melissa, Jenny, Therese, and Lyn. As always, my gratitude goes to the women at Naiad Press and to the person holding this book at this moment. There is no one I appreciate more than someone I have never met who sees one of my books on a shelf, takes it down, opens it, and starts to read.

About the Author

Julia Watts's first attempt at writing fiction came at the age of eight when she penned *The Tales of the Clark Family,* an unpublished collection of short stories that chronicled the adventures of a group of spunky orphans and that borrowed heavily from the plots of Charlie Brown holiday specials. She likes to think that since that first creative endeavor her writing technique has improved. A native of southeastern Kentucky, Watts holds an M.A. in creative writing from the University of Louisville and is a two-time recipient of the Kentucky Foundation for Women's grant for fiction writing. She is the author of three previous novels: *Wildwood Flowers, Phases of the Moon,* and *Piece of My Heart,* all of which were published by Naiad Press. Her other fiction has been published in the anthology *Countering the Myths,* the literary journal *The American Voice,* and various Naiad Press anthologies.

Chapter 1

"Widowhood may cause some major changes in my life, but it sure as hell won't affect my wardrobe," Lily muttered as she surveyed the dozens of black dresses in her closet. Of course, even though all of her dresses were black, most of them wouldn't be appropriate for the memorial service — or the funeral, as Charlotte's parents insisted on calling it.

The black minidress printed with images of Jackie O's face was definitely out, although Lily couldn't help but think that Charlotte — wherever she was — would get a kick out of seeing Lily show up at her memorial service in a dress paying tribute to that most famous of professional widows. Lily would have to wear something with long enough sleeves to cover her tattoos — the woman's symbol in Celtic knotwork she'd gotten on her right bicep to celebrate her lesbianism and the matching band in knotwork she'd gotten just below it, to mark her commitment to Charlotte.

After Lily and Charlotte had been together three years, they were surprised to find themselves yearning for a symbol of the permanence of their relationship. The media flooded consumers with images of heterosexual commitment: diamond engagement rings, virginal white wedding gowns, and honeymoon suites reserved for church-and-state–approved hetero hanky-panky. But for same-sex couples, symbols of commitment were hard to find.

They had toyed briefly with the ring—and-commitment–ceremony route but gave up the notion when they tried to picture themselves in a jewelry store, crooning over diamonds like a former frat boy and his bleached-blond bride-to-be. Besides, the only pieces of jewelry Lily wore regularly were the silver rings in her ears, nose, and navel, and Charlotte was a professed socialist who eschewed status symbols. Neither of them was the diamond-ring type.

And so they had settled on the armbands. The tattooing had been their commitment ceremony. Charlotte had held Lily's left hand while the lesbian tattoo artist inked her right arm, and Lily did the same for Charlotte when her turn came. After their artwork was complete, they had kissed.

That night, Lily and Charlotte had enjoyed a night of passionate but awkward lovemaking, as they

2

wallowed in connubial bliss while trying to avoid each other's bandaged biceps.

The past two weeks, the image of Charlotte's armband had haunted Lily. When the highway patrolman told her that Charlotte's car had been run off a rain-slick road in southern Georgia, Lily's mind flashed to Charlotte's tattoo. Charlotte had left the house the morning of the accident wearing a black T-shirt with the sleeves cut off so she could show off her ink and shock her uptight academic colleagues.

Later, when Charlotte's body was being cremated, Lily thought again of the tattoo, of the symbol of their love, burning away to ashes.

Maybe all couples should get tattoos as a sign of commitment, Lily thought as she yanked on the pantyhose she resented wearing. A wedding ring could be put in a drawer and forgotten after one's partner passed on, but a tattoo was a constant reminder to remember. No matter what happened, Lily would always be marked by Charlotte's love.

Lily regarded herself in the full-length mirror: her plain black vintage dress with its tattoo-concealing sleeves, her black stockings, and the black Mary Janes with chunky high heels, which were the closest thing to a respectable-looking pair of shoes she owned. She had pulled her white-girl dreadlocks into a messy bun so her hair didn't look too wild, and she had replaced the silver hoop in her nose with a tiny silver stud. She had considered removing her body jewelry altogether, but she couldn't bear to. Her multiple piercings were the only thing that prevented her from looking like someone's grandmother from the Old Country.

Lily walked to the room at the end of the hall,

where Mimi was still asleep in her crib. Lily hated to wake her up to take her to this damned thing. Charlotte's real funeral had been last week — a small, private service in which Charlotte's friends had gathered to remember Charlotte the way she really was. They had told stories and read poems by Adrienne Rich and Audre Lorde to the accompaniment of a softly strumming guitarist, and Lily had cried until she marveled that there was any fluid left in her body.

But today's service had nothing to do with Charlotte. Had she been alive, it would have been the kind of thing you couldn't have dragged her to. Today's service was about Charlotte's parents and how they wanted to remember her — which, of course, was in complete contrast to her. Now that Charlotte was dead, her parents could shape her into what they had always wanted her to be: a dutiful, passive, Christian daughter. Of course, the only reason they could make this transformation was that Charlotte was no longer around to defend herself.

But Lily was still around — a fact, she was sure, that troubled Charlotte's parents no end. And for as long as she was around, she would defend Charlotte's real memory. Charlotte's parents might not like it, but they would have to put up with Lily's troublemaking for one reason: Mimi, the bearer of Charlotte's genetic material, who was snoring sweetly in her crib.

The story of Mimi's conception, like the conception stories of all children of lesbian parents, was a long one. Lily and Charlotte had often discussed the fact that if straight couples had to go to the same trouble as lesbians to get pregnant, there would be fewer cases of abused and neglected children because there would be no instances of "oops, a pregnancy." Every child would be wanted because the parents would have gone to a whole hell of a lot of trouble in order to conceive.

Even though Mimi's conception was the result of many frustrating months and so many intimate encounters with a turkey baster that Thanksgiving would never be the same again, the method by which Mimi's biological parents were chosen had been as simple as a game at a children's party.

Lily and Charlotte's best friends were Desmond and Ben, who lived in the condo adjoining theirs. Ex-lovers whose personalities were as different as RuPaul's and Bruce Bawer's, Desmond and Ben had continued to share the same living quarters even after they had stopped sharing a bed. It was as if they had decided that now that they were no longer lovers, they would be brothers instead — with a special emphasis on sibling rivalry.

On the evening Lily and Charlotte had naively thought their baby's conception would take place, Lily had made a pan of her famous eggplant parmesan while Charlotte had gone out to buy the biggest jug of decent wine she could find. That night, after Lily, Desmond, Ben, and Charlotte had eaten dinner and swilled down enough wine to giggle away any awkwardness, Lily had set two black hats on the coffee table, one labeled *sperm* and one labeled *egg*. The slip of paper drawn from the *sperm* hat would determine the sperm donor; the *egg* hat would reveal the biological mom's identity. Since Lily and Charlotte's cycles were in sync, they figured they were equally likely to conceive.

"Who gets to pick?" Charlotte asked.

"Well, one of the boys should get to pick from the *sperm* hat," Lily said.

"You do it, Ben. I'm too nervous. I feel like I'm a game-show contestant or something," Desmond said, his amethyst pinkie ring glittering as he poured himself another glass of wine.

"Oh, for god's sake —" Ben closed his eyes, picked a slip of paper out of the hat, unfolded it, and glanced at it. "It's you, Dez."

Dez leaped out of his chair and began dancing around the room, singing, "I get to be the patriarch! I get to be the patriarch!" The sight was made all the more comical by the fact that Dez's large body was clothed in a purple flowered caftan at the time.

"Are you girls sure you want him to be the father?" Ben asked. "I mean, what if the kid turns out to be a boy? Do you really want a son prancing around with Dez's genetic material?"

"Oh, I want you to listen to *her*," Dez said. "Just because *she's* got a closetful of Tommy Hilfiger, she thinks *she's* the butch one." He turned to Lily and Charlotte. "Any objections to the kid calling me Big Daddy? It's what Ben used to call me . . . once upon a time."

Ben looked down to hide his red cheeks. "Shut up, Dez. It's the girls' turn to draw."

Lily held out the *egg* hat, and Charlotte shut her eyes, selected a slip of paper, and glanced at it. "Omigod! It's me!" she whooped.

Ben laughed. "The queen and the diesel dyke! What kinda morphodite are you two figuring on making?"

Lily smiled. "Fortunately, a normal child was never what we were shooting for."

"Well, I, for one, am completely comfortable with the idea," Dez said. "This child will be yet another fine collaborative effort between Dr. Charlotte Maycomb and Dr. Desmond Reed."

Colleagues at Atlanta State University, Charlotte and Dez had collaborated on a number of academic papers and one book, *The Lust That Dared Not Speak Its Name: A History of Nineteenth-Century British Homosexual Scandals*.

After another round of wine, Lily, Charlotte, and Dez retreated upstairs while Ben flipped on the TV to catch the financial report on CNN. Once they were upstairs, Lily presented Dez with a glass jar. "Oh, so now that you've wined me and dined me, you want me to put out, is that it?" he said.

"I guess that's about the size of it. Uh . . . maybe you'd like to use the spare bedroom. Charlotte and I will be in our room whenever you're, uh, ready."

"Give me that issue of *Premiere* with Mark Wahlberg on it, and I won't be a minute."

Four minutes later, Dez knocked on Lily and Charlotte's bedroom door. "Here it is, ladies — my cuppa, cuppa burnin' love."

Lily gingerly accepted the jar, and Desmond bowed out of the room, with the comment that he was confident they had things under control from there. Lily did her business with the turkey baster, and then Charlotte stood on her head because she had read somewhere that it aided conception.

But the evening of eggplant parmesan was not to be the night of conception. Only unlucky teenagers get pregnant after just one ejaculation. Soon Charlotte, Lily, and Dez had done the jar-and-baster routine so many times that they lost all their self-consciousness.

It became a running joke. One afternoon Lily had rung Dez and Ben's doorbell and greeted them with, "Excuse me, but could I trouble you for a cup of sperm?"

On their last attempt, Dez delivered his jar to their door and said, "This better do the trick. The hair I'm growing on my palms is starting to cause some painful friction."

It did the trick. And nine months later, little Artemesia Gentileschi Maycomb (Mimi for short) was born. Lily, Dez, and Ben were all present in the birthing room, although Ben had to excuse himself to throw up when he saw the placenta.

Charlotte and Dez had lived long enough to see Mimi's first birthday. And if it hadn't been for Dez's morbid fear of airplanes, they might be alive still. But Dez refused to fly, so if he and Charlotte were going to attend a conference, no matter how far away it was, they always rented a car. So instead of flying into Miami for the gay/lesbian studies conference, they drove, and the rainy roads of southern Georgia robbed Mimi of her Mommy and Dezzy, Lily of her lover and her friend.

Lily gently shook her daughter's shoulder. "Wake up, sweetie. Time to go see your grandma and grandpa." Who are batshit crazy, she thought, but obviously she wasn't going to say this to a one-year-old.

"Mama?" Mimi's blue eyes, the image of her mother's, were droopy with sleep. "Mick."

"I'll get you some milk, Mimi-saurus." She supposed it was lucky that Mimi had been weaned from breast milk just before her first birthday, since the only kind of milk Lily could provide for her came in a can.

She carried Mimi downstairs and heated up some formula. After Mimi had sucked it down, Lily changed her diaper and brushed through her unruly baby hair — more out of habit than because it did any good.

Lily sighed and wished for a drink, a joint, an excuse. But there was no time for the first two, and her mind was too clouded by grief to think up an excuse. She grabbed her car keys and Mimi's diaper bag.

It was time to go to church.

Chapter 2

Lily felt empty and unsettled as she drove out of downtown Atlanta and into Cobb County. She imagined it was much the same feeling native New Yorkers got when they crossed the line into New Jersey: the feeling of being among "them" instead of "us."

Downtown Atlanta had character, history, and the tolerant *do-what-you-want* quality of the city. Hole-in-the-wall Thai restaurants sat next door to gay leather bars. You could see the church once pastored by Martin Luther King, the Margaret Mitchell House, or (if your tastes ran to the morbid) the street corner where Ms. Mitchell was fatally hit by a taxi. The junk-food establishments even had character and history: the Varsity, where comedian Nipsy Russell had once worked as a carhop, and the Majestic, the seedy all-night diner where Jack Kerouac used to kill time.

Driving through Cobb County, though, it was rare to see buildings that had been erected prior to 1975. Restaurants consisted mainly of the usual suspects: McDonald's, Chuck E. Cheese, Steak 'n Shake. The stores were links in multinational chains and were housed in sterile strip malls. If someone blindfolded me and dropped me in the middle of Cobb County, Lily thought, there would be no way I could figure out where the hell I was. The area had no distinguishing characteristics.

Calvary Baptist Church, the church where Charlotte's family were having their little denial-fest of a memorial service, was the biggest, ugliest Protestant church on a street lined with big, ugly Protestant churches. Calvary was especially aesthetically offensive because of its puke-yellow brick and cream-colored, plantation-style columns. The plantation image was appropriate for the church, though, since the only black person ever seen on the premises was the janitor.

"Damn," Lily muttered when she saw that according to the church clock, she was five minutes late. According to her battered Timex, she was two minutes early, but apparently her watch didn't run on Cobb County time. She scooped Mimi up out of her car seat. "Okay, kid, you've never been to one of these before, and hopefully you'll never have to go to one again. It's called a church service."

11

Once inside, Lily followed the sound of the maudlin organ music and slipped into a back pew in the sanctuary. An old lady in a wig that was slightly askew pounded on the pipe organ — one of those droning songs from the *Baptist Hymnal*. Was it "Rock of Ages" or "Blessed Assurance"? Lily could never keep those oldies-but-oldies straight, and her memory wasn't aided by the fact that the goal of most WASP church musicians seemed to be to make all the songs sound as much alike as possible.

The stark white sanctuary was huge, but fewer than twenty people sat in the pews: Charlotte's parents, recognizable because of Ida Maycomb's helmet of rigidly coiffed brown hair and Charles Maycomb's shiny bald pate; Charlotte's brother Mike, there with his wife and two kids; and a few of Charlotte's aunts and uncles. Lily figured that the other people in attendance were the types who waited around for the church doors to be unlocked so they could dart in and warm a pew. If this had been a real memorial service, instead of Ida and Charles Maycomb's half-assed attempt to mark the passing of the daughter they never approved of, the turnout would have been pathetic.

After the pipe organ breathed its last, a puffy man whose gray hair matched his gray three-piece suit took his place behind the podium. "We gather here today," he said, his voice dripping with mock solemnity, "to mourn the passing of the daughter of two of our congregation's most beloved members, Ida and Charles Maycomb."

Lily saw where this was going. Charlotte wasn't even going to get top billing at her own memorial service.

"As Scripture has shown us," the reverend continued, "there are few experiences more painful than the death of a child. When God tests Job, he takes his children from him. And just as Job wept for his lost children, today we join Ida and Charles Maycomb in weeping for their lost child, Charlotte Maycomb."

Lily shifted Mimi's weight on her lap. Lost *child*? Charlotte had been thirty-eight years old.

"And as always, Charlotte's passing gives us the opportunity to ask ourselves: Are we really living our lives in a way that would make Jesus proud?" The rev was curiously puffy — not fat, exactly, but bloated, as though someone had given him an enema with the air from a bicycle pump. "Or when our time comes and we stand before Saint Peter at the pearly gates, are we going to have some explaining to do? Today, as we observe Charlotte's passing, I urge you all to think: If Jesus took you today, where would you spend eternity?"

Lily heard Ida's sobs. No doubt she was contemplating her sinful lesbian daughter frying extra-crispy in the fires of hell. Lily had no doubt that Charlotte's sinfulness was the not-so-subtle subtext of the rev's little sermon. What made it all the more irritating was his delivery. For some reason, Lily didn't object to the loud-mouthed hellfire-and-brimstone preachers as much as preachers like Mr. Calvary Baptist here. While the ideas he expressed were the same old damnation-and-judgment mambo, he spoke in sweet, subdued tones with a simper on his face that Lily longed to slap off. The only thing worse than regular hellfire and brimstone, Lily decided, was candy-coated hellfire and brimstone.

13

Lily spaced out for a few comparatively pleasant minutes, but when her attention returned to the gray three-piece suit behind the podium, he said, "And now, we're going to hear from somebody who holds our dearly departed in a very special place in his heart. I ask you: What can be more tender, more protective and sweet than a big brother's love for his little sister? Michael Charles Maycomb, won't you come up and say a few words?"

Mike? Lily nearly dropped the baby off her lap in shock. According to Charlotte, Mike had been intent on making Charlotte's life as unpleasant as possible from the moment she was born. When Charlotte was an infant, her baby skin was covered with bruises from where Mike used to pinch her when nobody was looking. When she was a little girl, Mike took the axe from the toolshed and chopped her new red wagon into splinters. When, as a young adolescent, Charlotte began to develop at a rapid rate, Mike insisted on calling her "Jugs." And this was only the stuff Charlotte had told Lily about. No matter what Mike did when they were growing up, Charlotte told Lily, her parents dismissed it with clichés like, "Boys will be boys."

Now Mike was president of the Cobb County chapter of the Lord's Lieutenants, an all-male Christian paramilitary organization devoted to preserving traditional Christian values, particularly as they pertain to the submission of women. Prior to her death, Charlotte only saw Mike at unavoidable family occasions. Once, Charlotte had told Lily, Mike had cornered her and told her how being the liberal she was, she should appreciate the Lord's Lieutenants because they happily accepted black, Latino, and Asian men into their ranks. Charlotte had replied, "How beautiful . . . all races, creeds, and colors united in the spirit of misogyny."

Charlotte told Lily afterward that she was sure this comment would have really pissed Mike off, if he had known what the word *misogyny* meant.

And so it was Mike whom the Maycombs had decided would memorialize Charlotte. It was fitting, in a perverse way. They never understood her while she was alive. Why should they understand her now that she was dead?

Mike stood at the lectern in his gray three-piece suit (What is it with the gray three-piece suits in this church? Lily wondered), his ash-blond hair combed over his bald spot. "Charlotte always did love reading literature and stuff like that," he began, "so I've composed a poem in her honor."

Dear god, no, Lily thought.

He cleared his throat and began. "It's called, 'My Sister'." He began reading in the sing-song rhythm that the marginally literate feel is integral to poetry:

When I was a boy, God looked down and saw
    me at my play.
He said, "This boy needs a friend to help him
    on his way."
That's why, I think, he saw fit to send you
    to me —
A little baby sister — as sweet as sweet could
    be.
I used to stand and watch you as in your crib
    you laid.
As time went by and you grew some, in the
    yard we played.

15

More time went by, and I admit, I was
  surprised to see
The educated lady that you turned out to be.
Now the Lord has taken you, and as we
  together pray,
There's something I have never said that I
  want to say.
Although I've never said it, please know that it
  is true,
When I say these three words, my sister: I . . .

Then a miracle occurred. Well, the closest thing to
a miracle this church would see anyway. As Lily held
the suddenly restless Mimi on her lap, she detected
warmth and movement emanating from the child's
diaper. Hallelujah! Lily thought. The child hath
pooped! Now I have a socially acceptable reason to
bolt from this debacle of a memorial service.

Just then, Mimi emitted an eardrum-shattering
wail. Given the nature of Mike's poem, Lily wasn't
sure if Mimi was crying because of her soiled diaper
or because she was a budding literary critic.

When Lily carried Mimi into the ladies' room, she
was dismayed to discover that it was not equipped
with a changing table. Great, she thought, all this talk
of family values in this church, and they don't even
give me a place to change a poopy diaper. She changed
Mimi awkwardly on the counter, and then noticed that
the large mirror above the counter protruded two or
three inches from the wall. Instead of throwing the
dirty diaper into the trash like a good girl, she
slam-dunked it so it wedged between the mirror and
the wall. By tomorrow morning's service, that diaper

would be stinking up the place pretty good, and they'd go nuts trying to figure out where the smell was coming from.

Lily reentered the sanctuary just in time to hear the rev suggest that they all join in singing "How Great Thou Art," since it had been "one of Charlotte's favorites." To the best of Lily's memory, Charlotte's favorite song had been Patti Smith's version of "Gloria."

As soon as the service was over, Ida made a bee-line for Lily. "There's my little precious!" she squealed at Mimi. "There's Grandma's little angel!"

"Gamma!" Mimi sprang into Ida's arms, and Ida carried her away without even acknowledging Lily's presence.

Lily watched as Ida showed Mimi off to her church friends. As she watched the bald men and shampooed-and-set women coo over her daughter, Lily was reminded of that scene in *Rosemary's Baby* where Rosemary discovers all the wrinkled old Satanists keeping watch over her baby's black bassinet. Five minutes, she thought. They can fuss over Mimi for exactly five minutes, but then we've got to get out of here before I turn into a pumpkin or a pillar of salt or something.

She watched the seconds tick by on her Timex, gnawed her already nubby fingernails, and thought how much Charlotte would have hated this whole thing. As she approached Ida and one of her church-lady friends, she heard the friend say, "Cremated? Really? Well, of course, I would just never feel right about being cremated, but Charlotte always was" — she stiffened when she saw Lily — "different."

"Mama!" Mimi called when she saw Lily. Lily was sure it wasn't her imagination that both Ida and her sour-faced friend cringed.

"I guess we'd better be taking off," Lily said.

"Ooh, can't this precious angel stay with her grandma just a few teeny-weeny minutes?"

Great, make me the bad guy, Lily thought. "Well, it is getting to be her dinnertime . . ."

"Oh, all right," Ida sighed, careful to hand over Mimi without making any physical contact with Lily — wouldn't want to catch those lesbian cooties. "But I think the boys had something they wanted to talk to you about before you left." She looked around in that desperate, dithering way she had, calling, "Charles! Mike! Lily's leaving!"

Charles and Mike appeared at her side. Charles nodded at Lily and said, "We'll walk you to your car."

Walking to the car with a large, gray-suited man on either side of her, Lily felt like she was in one of those scenes in a movie in which the mobsters politely escort their victim to a car with the destination of a deserted warehouse where no one can hear the screams.

When they reached her car, Charles said, "We didn't want to say anything at the reading of the will — didn't want to make a scene. We know how upset you were — how upset we all were." His tone was gentle, calm. "But we just wanted to let you know today, Mike here's been talking to some attorneys who are in the Lord's Lieutenants with him —"

"Attorneys?" Lily's stomach tied itself into a Gordian knot.

"Yes," Mike said. "You see, we just don't feel that a young lady on her own . . . a young lady such as

yourself, with no blood ties to Mimi whatsoever . . .
what kind of parent could you possibly be?"

"I've been a damned good one for the past thirteen
months." She ran her hand through her hair, which
loosened her bun and made her dreadlocks fall loose
on her shoulders. "Look, I don't have to justify myself
to you. You read Charlotte's will the same as I did. If
you loved Charlotte at all, you'd respect her wishes."

Charles's tone was irritatingly even. "We loved
Charlotte very much. It's just that we don't feel she
was capable of understanding what is best for her
child. She was blinded by her . . . her . . ."

"Her sickness," Mike finished helpfully.

Lily set Mimi in her car seat and spun around to
face her enemies. "Her sickness, huh? Let me tell you,
this, *this*, is the sick shit right here! Charlotte knew
more about loving and raising a child than you
fucking bigots ever did!"

"See, this is just the kind of thing we're talking
about," Mike said calmly. "You should never use such
foul language in front of a child." He pressed a card
into Lily's fist. "If you decide you'd like to talk
sensibly about this, you can speak to our attorney."

As Charlotte and Mike walked away, Lily looked at
the card in her hand: STEPHEN J. HAMILTON,
ATTORNEY-AT-LAW. Hamilton was one of the most
powerful right-wingers in the state. And all Lily had
on her side were the wishes of her dead lesbian lover.

She got in the car and pounded her head against
the steering wheel. That was productive, she thought.
Now what the hell am I going to do?

Chapter 3

Lily sat on the couch with her head on Ben's shoulder, a glass of wine in one hand and a Kleenex in the other. When she'd put Mimi to bed an hour ago, she had stood by her crib watching her sleep. Mimi was perfect in sleep — her fringe of eyelashes resting on her round cheeks, her little rosebud lips slightly parted. Lily had trembled with the fear of losing her.

Charlotte's absence left an aching void in Lily's life, but even the second Lily heard about the accident, she knew she would go on. She would have to, for Mimi. Without Mimi, though, Lily couldn't even imagine a reason for waking up in the morning, for keeping up a pretense of living.

Lily could tell that Ben wasn't used to women crying on his shoulder. He patted her in the distracted way a person who isn't particularly fond of dogs might pat an affection-starved beagle. "Fucking breeders," he muttered.

"Hey," Lily sniffed, "you promised Charlotte and me you wouldn't use that word anymore after we decided to have the baby."

"It's different with queers," Ben said. "You and Charlotte made an informed decision to become parents. Breeders litter the earth with their progeny without even giving it a thought. But even that's not enough for them; they have to take our kids, too."

Dez and Charlotte used to make fun of Ben's dismal views of the plight of gays. Dez always said Ben sounded like one of the tragic homos in those '50s pulp novels with titles like *Children of Twilight*. Today, though, Lily wondered if Ben's bleak view might be valid. She sniveled some more on his Tommy Hilfiger T-shirted shoulder, even though the way he was patting her was starting to get on her nerves.

"Okay, enough of this," Ben said abruptly. "My shoulder is falling asleep."

Lily sat up. "Sorry, man. Didn't mean to test the bounds of your sensitivity."

"I'm just trying to be practical. Crying gets us nowhere. We've got to decide what we're going to do."

"Do? There's nothing to do. I mean, I'll hire a gay-positive lawyer, and we'll go to court and everything. But we're doomed. Don't you know how every single custody case involving a lesbian mom has turned out?

21

Judges would rather see kids raised by a child-molesting serial killer than a dyke. And I'm not even Mimi's biological mother!"

Ben rose from the couch and started pacing. "Well, it certainly is a complex problem." He paced back and forth across the living room floor. "Hmm. Let me ask you this. You're not bound to Atlanta for any reason, are you? I mean . . . you could do your work somewhere else, right?"

Lily was the author and illustrator of several books for children. As long as she had her drawing board, she could work anywhere. Of course, the past couple of weeks, she hadn't felt much like working. "Sure . . . I guess I could go somewhere else." She tried to picture herself and Mimi and Ben on a cross-country trek, hiding from the Maycombs. "But Ben, I don't think we can run away from this, and if you'll forgive me for saying so, you don't exactly strike me as the *Thelma and Louise* type."

"You're right on that count. All I could think about the whole time I was watching that movie was how long it had been since those girls had taken a shower." He paced some more in silence, then asked, "What kind of relationship do you have with your family?"

"Not much of one. Mom and Dad are divorced. Dad and I exchange Christmas and birthday cards, and that's about it. Mom and I have lunch every couple of months or so. She tells me that I'm a grown woman and should get a decent hairstyle and take that ridiculous thing out of my nose."

"And if you mention your private life?"

"She sticks her fingers in her ears and sings 'Mary Had a Little Lamb.' When she has no choice but to acknowledge Mimi, she refers to her as 'your friend's daughter.' "

"Well, obviously we're not gonna get much help on that front."

Lily poured another glass of wine. "Ben, nobody's gonna help us except other queers, and nobody's gonna listen to them anyway 'cause . . . well, they're a bunch of queers." She slammed her wineglass so hard on the coffee table that the base broke, nicking her index finger. "Goddamn it!" She stuck her finger in her mouth and sucked.

"Are you okay?"

"No, I am most certainly not okay. My daughter is going to be raised by Republicans."

Ben sat down next to her. "Lily, I need to ask you a question."

"So ask." The cut on her finger was almost a relief — a small dose of physical pain to distract her from the pain that mattered.

"Okay, I'm very serious here. Would you do anything to keep Mimi?"

She didn't have to pause to think. "Yes. She's all I have left. If anything had a chance of working, I'd try it."

"Even if it meant putting yourself in a hellish situation?"

"In case you haven't noticed, buddy, I'm in a hellish situation right now. Stop being so damned mysterious. What are you thinking?"

Ben sighed. "Okay. My family — they drive me nuts, but they have the two things that might get us out of this situation."

"An AK-47 and what else?"

"Better than that. They have the two things in

this country that can get you out of just about any situation: money and power."

Lily had always known that Ben was on the payroll for some family business he rarely did any work for. The way Dez had told it, Ben's parents kept him paid off so he wouldn't come back to his small north Georgia hometown and flaunt his homosexuality. "But from what I've heard from you and Dez, your family hasn't exactly joined up with P-FLAG. Would they be willing to use their money and power to help us?"

"Under the right circumstances."

Lily smelled compromise — an odor she hated. But she had said she would do anything to keep Mimi, and she meant it. She took a deep breath. "And what circumstances would those be?"

"Okay," Ben began. "Suppose — just suppose for a second — that I'm actually Mimi's biological father."

"But we both know Dez is."

"For a writer, you're not being very imaginative. Let's say that unbeknownst to you and Dez, Charlotte and I were having an affair."

For the first time in two full weeks, Lily laughed out loud.

"I know. It's ridiculous. But remember: We're cooking up a story for the breeders. They want us to be straight so badly, they'll believe any bullshit story we come up with."

Lily cleared her throat to stifle a giggle. "So you and Charlotte were having an affair." She tried to imagine Charlotte and Ben locked in a passionate clench. "She was the top, obviously."

"Don't be ridiculous. I was the top. I'm the man,

aren't I?" His voice squeaked as he defended his masculinity.

"If you say so, dear."

"So anyway, Charlotte and I had been having this affair, and she tearfully confessed to me when she got pregnant with Mimi, that she was sure that I, not Dez, was the father ..."

"Where did you come up with this story, *Soap Opera Digest*?"

"We both know it's absurd, and Charlotte and Dez are probably giggling in their graves at the idea. But don't you think they'd want us to do whatever it took to keep their baby away from those Cobb County cretins?"

"Of course they would. I just don't see where this flight of fancy is taking us."

"Wake up and smell the patriarchy, Lily! If I can convince a jury that I'm Mimi's biological father, then I'll have a legitimate claim on her."

"But they can do tests for that kind of thing now, if the judge orders it. DNA ..."

"Which brings me to my family. My brothers were what you might call mischievous when they were growing up. Mother and Daddy bought them out of so much trouble with the law that they *own* the judge of the juvenile court in Faulkner County — he's practically a house pet. There's no way Judge Sanders is gonna make a member of the McGilly family take a DNA test. He knows a McGilly's word is as good as his next payoff."

"So how are we gonna manage to get this case tried in your hometown?"

"That's where we come to the part of the plan

that'll make the whole thing work." Ben cleared his throat and arched an eyebrow. "Lily, will you marry me?"

She had seen the question coming, but she still couldn't stifle her laughter. "I swore when I was in first grade I'd never marry a man."

"It wouldn't be like a real marriage. I'm not gonna take advantage of your virtue or anything. The one time I tried to have sex with a woman, I threw up on her." He sat back down next to Lily. "Here's what I'm thinking. We get married, we move to Faulkner County for the time being, convince my parents our marriage is the real thing, give them time to fall in love with Mimi. And that won't take any time at all, because they've got grandsons out the wazoo, but not one granddaughter. We'll have the case tried there, get joint custody of Mimi, then we can move back here to our respective condos. We can stay married for the insurance benefits or get a divorce, whichever you want."

Lily's heart was racing. "You make it sound so easy, but this . . . this goes against my whole personal philosophy." She rolled up her sleeve to show her woman symbol tattoo. "When I got this tattoo, I was nineteen years old. I swore then that I'd always be true to my lesbian identity . . . that I'd never closet myself, or use vague pronouns, or —"

"That's all very moving, hon. But is your pride worth allowing your daughter to be raised a Southern Baptist?"

Lily collapsed with her head in her hands. "Oh god."

"If it helps, you can think of this as a subversive

act. We'll not just be lying out of self-protection; we'll be beating the straight people at their own game."

Lily sat in silence for a moment. Hellish as the plan was, it was the only course of action she could think of that might give them a chance of success ... if they could pull it off. "I won't have to, like, wear a white dress or anything, will I?"

"Hell, no. We'll just have a justice of the peace do it. You can wear jeans and a Lesbian Avengers T-shirt for all I care. The thing is, though, in front of my folks and the judge, we'll have to make it look real. We'll have to be affectionate with each other, and in order to play well in Faulkner County, you'll have to take my name —"

Lily started laughing so hard she couldn't get her breath. Tears streamed down her cheeks.

"What is it?" Ben asked.

"I don't fucking believe it," she said when she could finally speak. "My whole life I've sworn never to let men influence my identity, and now I'm going to be named Lily McGilly."

Chapter 4

Ben's Lexus sped along the interstate, taking Lily into a world so different it was hard for her to believe they'd been in Atlanta a scant fifty minutes ago. The only traveling Lily had done in the past several years was for book signings. She'd drive to the Atlanta airport, board a plane, and be deposited into another metropolitan area. A native Atlantan, Lily had seen little of the expanses of country that lay between major metropolitan areas.

She looked behind her, where Mimi was snoozing away in her car seat. As always, Lily saw Charlotte's face in Mimi's. She hoped she was doing the right thing.

They passed a green sign that read FAULKNER COUNTY. "Last chance to back out," Ben said. His tone was only half-joking.

Lily replied, "I'm willing to go through with it if you are. Although I must admit I'm surprised you're willing to go so far to help Mimi. I mean, you don't even like kids."

"Look, I know I'm not the most touchy-feely person in the world, but Dez meant a lot to me. He brought me out into the gay world, and even after we weren't lovers, he was my best friend. Babies are noisy and erratic and have no control over their biological functions, but that baby in the backseat carries Dez's genetic material, and I'll be damned if I'm gonna see her raised in a way Dez would disapprove of."

"So," Lily said, "which are we gonna do first, go see your folks or get married?"

"Oh, get married, definitely. If we don't, Mom'll try to rope us into having a big church wedding, and I don't think either of us is up for that."

"God, no. Weddings are barbaric. I've never understood why people think they're romantic — all that heavy-handed symbolism about virginity and fertility . . . it's about as romantic as throwing a virgin into a volcano."

Ben laughed. "Well, we're lucky. In Faulkner County, they have this deal where you can get married in a day. The blood test, the license, the ceremony . . . you can get it all done in about an hour, if it's not too crowded."

"Instant heterosexual respectability in an hour, huh? Pretty amazing."

Ben put on his turn signal as they approached the exit sign marked VERSAILLES.

"Versailles?" Lily asked.

"Actually, everybody pronounces it *Ver-sales*. Trust me; it's more appropriate."

The interstate exit for Versailles was home to only two businesses, a ramshackle fruit stand selling Georgia peaches and boiled peanuts, and the Lazy J Truck Stop, which, according to its sign, offered both FRIED CHICKEN AND HOT SHOWERS.

Downtown Versailles was a scant block long. All the businesses seemed to be lost in the early '60s. The window of the La-Di-Da Dress Shop displayed pastel suits that looked like bargain basement versions of what the queen of widows had worn before she was given the moniker "Jackie O." Next door to the La-Di-Da, the Chatterbox Beauty Shop looked as though it might dole out hairdos to match the dress shop's anachronistic clothing.

The only downtown eating establishment was a diner called the Dinner Bucket. "You know," Lily said, "somehow I just don't find *bucket* to be a very appetizing word."

Ben pulled over in front of a squat brick doctor's office. "Yeah, it does sound kinda like slopping the hogs, doesn't it? And the really awful thing is that nobody in town calls it the Dinner Bucket — they just call it the Bucket." He put the car in park and looked in the direction of the doctor's office. "So . . . are you ready to bleed?"

"Do we need an appointment?"

"Nope. That's why you can get married in a day here. They've got a lab tech on staff whose only job is to draw the blood of the betrothed — no appointments necessary."

Mimi was sweaty and cranky from her nap in the car. As soon as Lily took her into the doctor's office, she got to work making her a juice bottle while Ben waited at the front desk to check in.

A heavy woman in a white polyester uniform emerged from behind the EMPLOYEES ONLY door and promptly crowed, "Well, Benny Jack McGilly, as I live and breathe!"

Lily stifled the guffaw she felt rising from her belly. *Benny Jack?* Mr. Tommy Hilfiger-wearing, *Wall Street Journal*-reading, Emory University alumnus over there was named Benny *Jack?*

"Hi, Maybelle. We need to get blood tests today."

Maybelle grinned. "Blood tests? Do you mean to tell me the oldest McGilly boy is finally getting married? I never thought I'd live to see the day!"

Ben glared up from the form he was filling out. "Believe me, neither did I."

"You having a big church wedding?" Maybelle asked, taking his paperwork.

"No. Actually, I'd really appreciate it if you didn't say anything about it. It's kind of a secret."

"A secret?"

Lily felt Maybelle's eyes on her as the chunky

woman suspiciously regarded Lily's nose ring and the baby on her lap. Lily gave the woman a jaunty wave, but it didn't seem to alter her opinion.

"A secret. I understand," Maybelle said.

Maybelle called Ben back first. Mimi was calmer now, sitting in the chair next to Lily and playing with her toy camera. There was precious little in the waiting room to keep patients amused: ancient copies of *Field and Stream* for the menfolk, equally antiquated issues of *Good Housekeeping* for the ladies. The kiddies were expected to amuse themselves with the *Children's Illustrated Bible*, the cover of which depicted an Aryan-looking Jesus talking to an equally Aryan-looking group of children.

In the lab, Lily sat down on a stool with Mimi on her lap. Although she was sure that Mimi was too young to comprehend what had happened to her mother, Lily had noticed that since the accident Mimi had clung to her like a baby koala bear. Tiny though she was, she seemed to sense that she had already lost one of her mothers and that she needed to be extra-careful not to lose this one, too.

The lab technician swabbed Lily's arm with alcohol and nodded at Mimi. "That Benny Jack's little girl?"

Lily reminded herself that this was the lie she was supposed to be perpetuating. She was going to have to be careful to keep her story straight. A lifetime of honesty hadn't prepared her for this kind of skullduggery. "Uh, yes," she said.

"I thought so," the lab tech replied. "She looks just like him."

Sure, lady. Whatever, Lily thought. But she smiled benignly. "Let's see. I guess you'll have to put your little girl down while I draw your blood. She can crawl around on the floor; she won't hurt nothin'."

Lily set Mimi down and turned her head as the needle entered her non-tattooed arm. Tattoo needles, she could handle. But she hated having blood drawn.

As Lily queasily watched the syringe fill with red fluid, a middle-aged, smiling nurse stuck her head in the door. "Hi, honey," she said to Lily. "I just wanted to stop by to ask if you had any questions about . . ." She pursed her lips demurely. "Married lady things. I've got all kinds of pamphlets, if you need 'em."

"Mama!" Mimi squealed happily. Despite the lab tech's certainty that she wouldn't "bother nothing," Mimi had managed to dump an entire bag of cotton balls on the floor and was petting them as if they were kittens.

The nurse looked at the baby, then at Lily. "I guess you won't be needing any pamphlets, will you, hon?" She scurried off.

"Poor ole Bernice," the lab tech said, sticking a round band-aid on Lily's arm. "She just can't get it through her head that there ain't a girl alive these days that needs one of her little pamphlets on what a girl should expect on her wedding night."

Lily laughed. "I guess girls are more sophisticated these days." More sophisticated than you'll ever know, she was thinking. "I'm sorry my daughter wrecked your lab."

"Oh, don't worry a thing about it. She's just as cute as she can be. If you and Benny Jack wanna check back in half an hour, we should have your test results ready."

After a quick trip to the Piggly Wiggly for cold

Cokes and Pampers, Ben and Lily returned to the doctor's office. "Congratulations!" Maybelle crowed when they walked in. "Y'all are healthy and compatible."

At the sound of the word *compatible*, Ben and Lily both burst out laughing.

The Faulkner County Courthouse was typical of small-town courthouse architecture: brick, columns, clock tower. In a stark, fluorescently lighted office, Lily and Ben waited for their license to be processed along with another soon-to-be wed couple. The man looked to be in his late thirties. His beard and mustache were tinged with gray. His bride-to-be, however, couldn't have been more than sixteen years old. She was big-eyed and bony except for her belly, which was swollen with pregnancy. The girl nodded at Mimi, who was standing up while holding onto Lily's knee. "How old?" the girl asked.

"Thirteen months," Lily said. "She's working on learning how to walk."

"She's pretty," the girl said, with a wistful smile on her face. "I can't wait til my baby comes, so I can play with him."

Lily smiled at the girl, but looking at her made her sad — this little girl who was going to play with her baby like a new doll. Lily couldn't even look at the grown man who had taken his bride's girlhood away.

Finally the clerk returned with Ben and Lily's paperwork. "There ya go," she said brightly, "and congratulations."

Lily was exhausted from hauling Mimi around. "So, where do we go to get this thing over with?"

"Over to the City Drug," Ben said. "The pharmacist there's the justice of the peace."

Lily followed him down the stairs. "We're getting married in a *drug* store?"

"Yup."

"Well, it's handy, I guess. We can get married and buy condoms for our wedding night in the same convenient location."

Ben stumbled on the stairs, steadied himself on the railing, and looked back at Lily with an expression of animal terror.

"I was joking! God."

The old lady in the half-glasses at the City Drug eyed Ben. "You're Big Ben McGilly's boy, ain'tcha?"

"Yes. Uh, and we're here to get married."

"A McGilly getting married in the City Drug? I've never heard the like! Why, when your little brother got married, they had it over at the country club. I heard tell they floated candles and flowers in that pond out by the golf course —"

"I know," Ben said impatiently. "I was there. The thing is, we're in kind of a hurry."

The woman looked Lily up and down. "I don't see why. She ain't showing yet. And that little girl's just about big enough to be a flower girl." When neither Lily nor Ben responded, she shrugged and hollered, "Frank! Wedding!"

"Bring 'em on back," a gruff voice called from the back of the store.

Frank was a paunchy, middle-aged guy in a too-tight pharmacist's smock. "Y'all got your license?" Ben presented the paperwork, and Frank glanced over it disinterestedly. "All right, then. Let's get started. Doris, you wanna witness?"

Doris, the lady in the half-glasses, presented Lily with a bouquet of red plastic carnations — the kind that would decorate graves in a cemetery near a trailer park. "A bride needs a bouquet," the old lady said, beaming.

And a blushing bride Lily was, with a baby in one arm and a tacky plastic bouquet in the other, wearing her Good Vibrations T-shirt, cutoff Levi's, and Doc Martens. If there were a magazine called *Postmodern Bride*, she would be its cover girl.

"Ben McGilly, do you take this woman, Lily Fox, to be your lawful wedded wife, to have and to hold, in sickness and in health, as long as you both shall live?" Frank droned. Clearly this ceremony was no more magical for him than it was for the bride and groom.

"Sure, okay," Ben said. "I do."

"Lily Fox, do you take this man, Ben McGilly . . ." While Frank finished his litany, Lily's eyes wandered to a nearby display shelf where she saw a box marked MEDICATED DOUCHE. When Frank finished the as-long-as-you-both-shall-live bit, Lily replied, "I . . . I douche," and collapsed in a fit of nervous giggles.

"Then you may kiss the bride." Frank apparently hadn't even heard her joke. Heterosexuals were a humorless lot, Lily decided.

Ben leaned over to kiss Lily's cheek, but she turned so he caught her on the lips. He was the one who had said they had to make this look real, after all. The kiss was completely bland, like pecking an old aunt's powder-scented jowl.

"Smile!" Doris said after their perfunctory kiss. She snapped a Polaroid of the three of them. Mimi was chewing on the plastic bridal bouquet. Doris handed the Polaroid to Ben. "Something to show your grandchildren."

"Thanks." Lily threw the god-awful snapshot in the trash as soon as they were out of the store. "That was certainly romantic," Lily muttered, strapping a complaining Mimi into her car seat. "It's okay, honey," she cooed to the little girl, "you won't be in your nasty old car seat much longer, I promise."

Ben started the car. "So . . . ready to go meet the in-laws?"

"Why not? Might as well make this day as surrealistic as possible." Today had been like a dream for Lily, though not in the sense that bubbly straight girls might say their wedding day was like a dream. Just like in her dreams, today Lily had been performing one bizarre action after another, and as in the dream world, no matter how bizarre her actions were, she had no choice but to perform them.

Ben drove them into the rolling hill country outside of Versailles, where the only businesses were the beautiful working farms and the ugly corrugated aluminum buildings that housed textile companies. Ben slowed down when they passed one of these buildings. "Well," he said, "there's the source of the fortune you just married into."

The slate-blue aluminum building hardly looked like the source of a family fortune. On the building's side was a block-lettered sign reading THE CON-

FEDERATE SOCK MILL. Next to the lettering was a line drawing of a cartoon Confederate soldier, who resembled a Civil War–era Beetle Bailey, leaning against a cannon, asleep in his sock feet. "Well . . ." Lily searched desperately for something to say.

"I know it doesn't look like much," Ben said. "But we do an incredible international business. You see, back when he was playing sports in high school, Daddy got frustrated because he couldn't find any socks that didn't start sagging after several washings. So after he graduated from technical school, he developed a special kind of elastic and patented it. Confederate Socks never lose their elasticity, and we've made millions off 'e. Daddy always gives free socks to the Faulkner County High football and basketball teams, since that was where his idea began."

"It's quite an American success story," Lily said. "Growing up with a self-made man like that for a dad, no wonder you vote Republican."

"Hey, it's in my best interest to make sure business is protected."

"Well, it may be in your best interest financially, but I still think that gay Republicans are like gazelles who try to make friends with lions." She and Ben had had this argument umpty-dozen times. "But I guess there's no need for us to argue politics on our wedding day, is there, honey?"

"I guess not . . . pumpkin."

Lily laughed. "So, how are your parents gonna take this — you showing up with new wife and baby in tow?"

"Oh, they'll be thrilled, once they get over the initial shock. I mean, you're certainly not who they would've picked out for me if they had had the choice,

38

but as far as their gay-boy son goes, any woman is better than no woman."

Lily looked up from gnawing her nails. "You sure know how to flatter a girl."

Right past a run-down store advertising live bait and sandwiches, Ben pulled into a long driveway. The driveway ended at a huge monstrosity of a house — a red brick mansion with antebellum columns and a cupola on the roof. "When Daddy had this house built, Mom couldn't decide if she wanted Tara or Monticello," Ben said, "so they kinda built both."

Lily wondered what she would do if she had the money to build a house like this. The only thing she knew for sure was that if she did, she definitely would not use the money to build a house like this.

"So," Ben said, "you ready to meet the folks?"

"Sure thing, Benny Jack."

"Never call me that. Half the reason I moved away from this damn place was so nobody would call me that."

Lily, with Mimi in her arms, followed Ben up the front porch steps. Ben opened the front door and hollered, "Mom!" There was no answer, so they went inside.

The living room was decorated in slate blue and mauve, with lots of geese, sheep, and other ersatz "country" doodads. A TV with a theater-sized screen dominated the room. "Mom!" Ben yelled again, then said, "She must be out back."

Lily followed Ben through the enormous kitchen, through the formal dining room with the fully stocked china cabinet and floral centerpiece on the table, through the sunroom with its white wicker furniture.

They went out the back door and down a stone path that led to a high wooden fence. Ben opened the gate.

Mrs. McGilly was lying on a floating air mattress in the Olympic-size swimming pool, reading a glossy-covered romance novel and eating grapes. She was an attractive woman, with curly light brown hair that was highlighted with the occasional streak of silver. For the mother of three grown children, her body was positively streamlined in her purple swimsuit.

Ben stood silently, waiting for her to notice him. Finally, she looked up and exclaimed, "Benny Jack! You 'bout scared me to death. You didn't tell me you was coming!"

"I wanted it to be a surprise."

Mrs. McGilly pulled down her sunglasses and regarded Lily and Mimi. "Well, hon, ain't you gonna introduce me?"

"Uh . . . sure, Mom. This is Lily, my wife, and Mimi, my daughter."

Mrs. McGilly sat bolt upright, upsetting the air mattress, and fell into the pool with a splash — sun-glasses, grapes, romance novel, and all.

Chapter 5

"I didn't mean to act so shocked," Mrs. McGilly said, as they sipped lemonade in the living room. "It's just that from the time he was a little boy, we never thought Benny Jack was the marrying kind."

"Well, I guess he just had to meet the right woman." Trying to act extra-wifely, Lily reached for her husband's clammy hand. She could tell that Ben was offended by his mother's insinuation about his proclivities. Despite Ben's rather obsessive penchant for color coordination, he liked to think he could pass for a hetero he-man.

"And I just can't believe this precious little doll here is my grandbaby!" Mrs. McGilly bounced the giggling Mimi on her knee. "Mamaw just can't wait to take her little granddaughter shopping, no, she can't." She looked up at Ben and Lily. "Of course, I'm absolutely scandalized that y'all got married at the City Drug. Why, we coulda had the biggest wedding Faulkner County's ever seen."

"You know I hate stuff like that," Ben said. "Besides, we thought a discreet marriage would be more appropriate — what with Mimi and all."

"Now, Benny Jack, you know good and well nobody in this town woulda said a thing about it if you'd had a big church wedding. You're a McGilly!" She smiled at Lily. "And now, so are you. We're glad to have ya, hon."

"Thank you, Mrs. McGilly."

"Now you're gonna have to drop that formal stuff. You're family now. The least you can do is call me Jeanie."

"Okay, Jeanie." Lily was finding it impossible not to like Jeanie McGilly. Despite the wealth that the obscene diamonds on her fingers attested to, she was completely devoid of pretension. Her attitude said: My husband and I worked damn hard for all this money, and by god, we're gonna enjoy it.

"You know what we oughta do tonight?" Jeanie said. "We oughta have a big barbecue to announce your marriage. Y'all are gonna be in town for a while, right?"

"Actually," Ben said, "we were talking about getting a place here."

Jeanie clapped her hands with little-girl delight. "Oh, nothing would make me happier than having all my boys right here in Versailles, all my grandbabies here where I can spoil 'em rotten!" She ran a French-manicured finger under her eyes. "Lord, I'm fixing to cry."

Lily was beginning to wonder how a person as open and natural as Jeanie could have produced a son as stuffy and uptight as Ben. "Well," said Lily, "I guess we should see about finding a motel —"

"Motel!" Jeanie yelped, as if the word were blasphemy. "No family of mine ever stays at a motel when they can stay with me." She leaned over conspiratorially. "Besides, hon, the only motel in Versailles is that run-down motor court on the old road, and they just rent rooms by the hour. Why don't y'all get your things, and I'll get you settled in the guest room? I would put you in Ben's old room, but I don't guess a new wife wants to spend the night in a room where she's looking at her husband's old math team trophies."

Lily had brought minimal luggage: a small suitcase stuffed with clean underwear, a couple of pairs of jeans, a few T-shirts, and two respectable dresses and a dressy pair of shoes for the inevitable court appearances. A single diaper bag filled with clothes and a few books and toys took care of Mimi's needs. Ben, by contrast, had brought two enormous suitcases that had to be pulled on wheels and one garment bag. They were certainly doing their job to defeat gender stereotypes.

"This is the grandkids' room," Jeanie said, showing them a bedroom crowded with two sets of bunk beds, a crib, and a playpen. "You know, I was just thinking this morning that I should get rid of that crib and playpen 'cause the boys is all getting so big." She tickled Mimi's chin. "I didn't know this mornin' that I was fixing to have me a baby granddaughter." She set Mimi down in the playpen, which was filled with colorful blocks and beads. "Why don't you play in here while I show Mommy and Daddy their room?"

Mommy and Daddy, Lily thought. Naturally, Jeanie thinks I'm Mimi's biological mother. She knew this was a notion they'd have to straighten out, but now didn't seem like the time.

"Oh, Lily, I wanna show you somethin'." Jeanie escorted her into a bathroom that was quite possibly the most sensual room Lily had ever seen. A deep marble tub, which was big enough to comfortably hold at least two people, was sunken into the floor. The tub was surrounded by candles, and a crystal bowl of many-colored bath oil beads sparkled like jewels in the light that shone through the window.

"What a beautiful bathroom," Lily said.

"You can use it any time you want to," Jeanie replied. "It's my special place, I guess. I've been with Benny Jack's daddy thirty-four years, and I've raised up three boys in this house. Sometimes I just need a place where I can get away from the men, you know what I mean?"

"I know exactly what you mean." Lily bit her lip as Ben erupted in a fake coughing fit.

"Well, this can be y'all's room." Jeanie led them into a room with a king-size canopy bed. Paintings of outdoor scenes hung on the cream and hunter-green striped walls, and a stuffed wild turkey stood guard in the corner, looking as if he might say, "Nevermore."

"Benny Jack's daddy bagged him a coupla years back," Jeanie said, when she caught Lily staring at the dead bird. "All the McGilly boys love to hunt, 'cept for Benny Jack here."

"Well, I wouldn't want him to hunt anyway," Lily said. "I'm an animal lover."

"And this way you won't be a widow during hunting season." Jeanie smiled. "Well, I'll let y'all get settled in. I'd better be heading to the store if we're gonna have a barbecue tonight."

Lily had already popped open a Bud tallboy before she realized that only the men were drinking beer. The women at the poolside barbecue appeared to be sticking to diet soft drinks. Ben's brothers, Johnny and Wayne, were knocking back beers and laughing, threatening to push one another into the pool. Lily couldn't help but observe how muscular both of Ben's bathing-suited brothers were. With their bulging biceps and V-shaped torsos, they would have been the gods of the gay scene if they had shared their brother's sexual orientation.

Ben stood with his buff brothers, looking unamused at their high jinks. He was the only male at the party drinking Diet Coke instead of beer.

Johnny and Wayne had five kids between them — scrawny, unruly boys between the ages of four and ten. Mimi sat on a beach towel, playing with her nesting cups and occasionally looking up at her new cousins' antics with the critical gaze of an anthropologist.

"You come on over here, Lily," Sheila, Wayne's wife, said. "Me and Tracee wanna give you a crash course on how to handle a McGilly man."

Lily managed a smile, knocked back some beer, and sat down at the redwood picnic table across from the other McGilly wives. Lily could tell she was going to have a hard time telling Sheila and Tracee apart. They both had dark tanning-bed tans and peroxided blond hair. Their aerobicized bodies didn't pooch or dimple in their bathing suits, and diamond rings and pendants glittered against their brown skin. They were the kind of girls who had made Lily's life hell in high school.

"So . . ." Sheila purred, "how did you meet Ben?"

"Through a mutual friend." It was true. Dez had been dating Ben at the time he and Charlotte started collaborating on papers. To celebrate the publication of Dez and Charlotte's first paper, the four of them had met for dinner at an Indian restaurant one night. Lily could have gone into detail about her and Ben's first meeting, but she figured the best policy here was not to lie unless it was absolutely necessary and to never give any more information than the bare minimum. "We were friends for a long time before we got . . . involved."

"Is that a fact?" Tracee laughed. "I had Johnny engaged to me before he knew what hit him. And of course, we had John Junior seven months after the wedding, so I don't guess I can say much about your little un over there being born outta wedlock. Me and Johnny just got in under the wire ourselves."

Lily smiled politely and took a big swig of beer.

"So, Lily, let's see your ring," Sheila said.

Lily looked down at her hands — so different from Sheila's and Tracee's well-manicured, gold-encrusted ones. Lily had artist's hands — long, callused fingers with nubby nails and ink stains that never quite washed away. "My ring?"

"You know," Sheila enunciated as though she were talking to a particularly slow-witted child, "your *diamond*. That Ben bought you."

"Oh," Lily said, "we haven't bought a ring yet."

"But, Lil-eeee!" Sheila whined. "You absolutely have to make him buy you a ring. That's one of the fun parts of being married. And let me tell you, you better enjoy the fun stuff while you can, because most of the time, being married'll just make you wanna tear your hair out!" Despite Sheila's words of doom, a smile was plastered across her face as she studied the enormous diamond that winked like a third eye on her hand.

"Well, I guess I'm just not that interested in material things," Lily said.

Sheila and Tracee wouldn't have looked at Lily with more shock if she had just confessed to being a serial killer.

Jeanie and an old woman Lily assumed was Ben's grandmother were arranging a buffet on a folding table. "Wayne!" Jeanie hollered. "I reckon you'll have to put the ribs on the grill. There's no telling when your daddy'll get home."

The old woman stuck a serving spoon in a bowl of potato salad and then made her way to the table where the McGilly wives were seated. "Oh, lord," Tracee muttered, "here she comes."

"Honey," the old woman said to Lily, "I just wanted to welcome you to the family. I'm Benny Jack's Granny McGilly."

"It's a pleasure to meet you, Mrs. McGil —"

"Now, there ain't no sense in you calling me Mrs. McGilly when your name's Mrs. McGilly, too." She grinned, revealing a mouthful of sparkling dentures. "Lily McGilly — that's a real humdinger of a name, ain't it? You must love my grandson something fierce to let yourself get saddled with a name like that!"

Lily laughed. "Well, that was the first thing I thought of when he proposed — if I could actually stand to go through life as Lily McGilly."

The old woman smiled back at her. "Well, Lily McGilly, you just call me Granny, you hear?"

"I will. Thank you." Granny McGilly was a stout old woman with soft white hair cut close to her head. She wore a plain blue T-shirt, sweatpants, and a pair of expensive white running shoes. Far from being a prissy old lady, she had an easy, comfortable manner about her that was almost butch. Lily liked her immediately.

"Well," Granny said, glancing over at the food table, "Wayne's got the meat on the grill and everything else is ready. I reckon I could set a spell." She sat down at the table next to Lily and across from Sheila and Tracee.

Sheila and Tracee exchanged glances, and Sheila said, "Excuse us. I think we're going for a swim."

When Sheila and Tracee got up, Granny said, "Lord, Sheila, that bathing suit you got on's crawling right up the crack of your hind end!"

"Everybody's wearing suits like this this season," Sheila said defensively. She turned to go to the pool, revealing most of her tanned, taut butt.

"She's just showing off," Granny whispered to Lily. "She had that thing done where they take a vacuum cleaner and suck all the fat outta your butt — what's that called?"

"Liposuction?"

"Yeah, that's it." Granny grinned. "Of course, she didn't have that much fat in her butt in the first place. If she'd had the fat sucked outta her head, that doctor woulda had a real job to do."

Lily laughed and looked down at Mimi, who started laughing, too.

"You know," Granny said, "you're the first woman I've ever seen drinking a beer at a McGilly barbecue. I think I just might have me one, too."

Granny grabbed a beer from the cooler while Lily watched Sheila and Tracee in the pool. They were staying at the shallow end — no doubt so they could avoid wetting their carefully coiffed hair. Of course, given Lily's recent conversation with the other McGilly wives, she thought the shallow end was an appropriate place for them.

"What's your baby's name?" Granny asked.

"Mimi — it's short for Artemesia."

Granny looked down at Mimi. "That's an awful big name for such a little-bitty girl. Benny Jack her daddy?"

"Uh-huh." Maybe she'd have another beer. The alcohol seemed to make lying easier — and it also eased the awkwardness of social interaction. Before her normal life had been interrupted, Lily had been a reclusive sort, content to spend her days bent over her drawing board, rising only to see to Mimi's needs, until Charlotte came home from work. Lily had probably talked to more people in the past two weeks than she had in the past two years.

"Benny Jack's the only one that's been able to make a baby girl," Granny said. "His brothers is just too all-boy, I reckon. I always did love me a little girl, though. You care if I hold her?"

"Go right ahead." Lily helped herself to a second beer.

Granny knelt down and made eye contact with Mimi. "Hey, Mimi, you care to come sit in an old woman's lap?"

Mimi smiled and raised her arms in the universal "pick-me-up" symbol.

"What's all this about?" a male voice boomed.

Lily looked up to see a middle-aged man, balding, bearded, and broad-shouldered, with a sizable paunch beneath his plain white T-shirt. She knew immediately that he was "Benny Jack's" father, Big Ben.

Jeanie ran over to stand at his side. "I thought about calling you at work to tell you, but I thought it'd be more exciting to surprise you at home." She looked across the pool. "Benny Jack! Come tell Daddy your news!"

Lily considered joining Ben but decided to stay put until she was told otherwise. From her safe spot at the picnic table, she heard Ben say, "Daddy, I'm married."

When Big Ben could close his jaw enough to speak, he shouted, "Married? To a woman?" Big Ben cackled with joy. "Hot damn! I never thought I'd live to see the day." He punched his son on the shoulder so hard that Ben lost his footing for a second. "Where is she? Where's the little lady?"

This, Lily guessed, was her cue. She rose. "Right here," she said.

Big Ben gallumphed over and placed a hand on each of her shoulders. "I don't believe I've ever been so happy to see a woman in my whole life."

Lily guessed that Ben had been right. Her nose ring, her dreadlocks, and her Doc Martens were irrelevant; the only thing that mattered to the McGillys was that she was a woman, and Ben had married her. "It's nice to meet you, Mr. —" She stopped herself. "Big Ben."

"Gan!" Mimi babbled from Granny McGilly's lap. She was already trying to say *granny*.

Big Ben looked down at the baby girl, surprised. "Now who is this?"

"This," Ben said, "is my daughter."

Big Ben looked at Mimi, then at Lily, and finally at Ben. His lips spread into an impossibly wide grin. He punched his son on the shoulder again. "You dog," he laughed. "You ole dog, you!"

The party was dying down. Wayne and Sheila and Johnny and Tracee had taken their kids home to bed. Jeanie and Granny were in the kitchen, washing the dishes after having assured Lily that there was no need for her to help them. "No need for a girl to wash dishes on her wedding night," Jeanie had said. "They'll be plenty of time for that kinda thing later, believe me."

51

Lily and Ben sat beside the pool with Big Ben, who was holding the sleeping Mimi in his arms. "Lily," he said, "I know I oughta let you put this baby girl to bed, but I swear, I don't believe I can stand to part with her."

"She does look awfully comfortable," Lily said. Big Ben cradled Mimi's little body in his enormous forearm and hand. In his other hand, he held the last beer from the cooler.

"Daddy," Ben said, "there's something I need to talk to you about . . . some legal trouble."

Big Ben raised his wooly eyebrows. "You in trouble with the law, boy?"

"No, Daddy . . . nothing like that. It's about Mimi, actually."

"Now you got me real confused, Benny Jack." Big Ben took another swig of beer and looked down at Mimi's cherubic face.

"It's about who gets custody of Mimi," Ben the younger said. "You see . . . I'm Mimi's biological father, but Lily here isn't Mimi's real mother."

Lily was offended by the phrase *real mother*, but decided it was best not to make an issue out of it . . . not while they were trying to make their case. "Mimi is the daughter of my best friend Charlotte," Lily explained. "She was killed in an accident, and she left custody of Mimi to me."

"Charlotte was in the car with Dez," Ben added.

Big Ben shook his head. "I sure was sorry when ole Dez got killed. He was queer as a three-dollar bill, but he was funny as hell." He stared off in the distance for a second. "Now, Benny Jack, Mimi here's your baby by Charlotte?"

"Yes. Charlotte and I were . . . involved."

Lily could tell she really wanted this plan to work because she managed to keep a straight face during this part of the story.

"Well, I'll be a monkey's uncle!" Big Ben laughed, obviously delighted. "All this time I thought you was a fairy, and here you was, with *two* women!"

"Go figure," Ben replied lamely.

"So, anyway," Lily said, "now Charlotte's parents want to contest my custody of Mimi — they don't think I should be allowed to raise her."

Big Ben drained his can of beer and crushed it. "Now is that on accounta them thinking there was somethin' between you and Charlotte?" His steel-gray eyes were focused on Lily.

"Well, uh . . . there was something between Charlotte and me," Lily said, as Ben shot her a warning glance. "But that was before I met Benny Jack here."

"Hmm." Big Ben scratched his beard thoughtfully. "Well, I don't even pretend to understand what it is you young people do today, but what I want to know is this: The two of y'all has a real marriage, right? You're devoted to each other, with no hanky-panky on the side?"

"We are," Ben and Lily said in unison.

"And y'all wanna make a real family for this little girl?"

"Yes."

"All right, then. First thing in the mornin', I'll get ole Buzz Dobson on the phone . . . he's our family lawyer. And Lily, you just tell Charlotte's parents to come on down to the Faulkner County Courthouse, and we'll have a big can o' whupass waitin' for 'em."

* * * * *

Lily and Ben lay in their marital bed, not consummating a thing. "You think you're gonna be able to do this?" Ben asked.

"Do what?" Lily gasped. She was a little nervous about his question, given where they were.

"Fake this whole marriage act for as long as it takes?"

"I think so. It's awfully fucking weird, though. This whole day has reminded me of when I was experimenting with hallucinogens in college."

"I know what you mean — not about the drugs, but about the weirdness. Tomorrow we'll see if we can rent an apartment . . . that way we'll be out from under my parents' watchful eyes. Plus, we won't be stuck in the same bed."

"That'd be cool. This isn't so bad, though. When I was little I used to sleep in the same bed with my cousins. It's kinda like that." She listened to her stomach rumble. "One thing we're definitely gonna have to do tomorrow is find some food I can eat. The only thing I could eat at the barbecue was that fruit salad with the little marshmallows in it."

"Yeah, my folks aren't much on vegetarian cuisine."

"No shit. Even the potato salad had bacon in it." They lay in awkward silence for a few minutes until finally Lily said, "Good night, husband."

"Good night, wife."

Lily closed her eyes and slept the sleep of exhaustion.

Chapter 6

Mimi had gone to the park with Dez. Finally, Lily and Charlotte could have some time alone. Since Mimi had come onto the scene, time alone *had become Charlotte and Lily's euphemism for the lovemaking that occurred all too infrequently between them. Their nighttime attempts at intimacy were often interrupted by Mimi howling for formula or climbing out of her crib to scratch pathetically at their bedroom door. As a result of this syndrome of caught-us-interruptus, Dez had agreed to take Mimi out for a couple of hours every two weeks so the women could enjoy some uninterrupted time alone.*

Although sex had become less frequent since Mimi's arrival, the rule seemed to be quality over quantity. Lily and Charlotte craved their time alone — ached for those couple of hours when they could be free of the responsibilities of mommyhood and lose themselves in each other.

Lily was aware of Charlotte behind her as they walked upstairs to the bedroom. Her breath caught in anticipation of what they were about to do. She let Charlotte follow her into the bedroom, taking pleasure in the fact that there was no need to close the door behind them.

Lily lay on the bed, barefoot in the little black dress she knew Charlotte liked, and watched Charlotte take off her watch and rings and set them on the bureau. Charlotte looked at Lily sprawled on the bed and smiled.

"C'mere," Lily coaxed, scooting over to make room.

"Just a second. I want to look at you first."

Lily laughed. "You look at me all the time."

But I never tire of it."

Lily lay on the bed, feeling Charlotte's gaze burn through her. In everyday life, Lily felt she was passably attractive in a sloppy, bohemian kind of way, but she certainly wasn't the kind of person who turned heads — male or female.

In the world of their bedroom, though, Charlotte made Lily feel like a high-femme fantasy figure. In Charlotte's eyes, in Charlotte's hands, she was Rita Hayworth . . . Marilyn Monroe.

When Charlotte finally joined Lily on the bed, their

56

lips met in a fierce, bruising kiss. Lily wrapped her arms and legs around her lover, who pressed down on her, as each of them tried to get as close to the other as possible.

Charlotte pulled down the shoulder strap of Lily's black dress and kissed her from shoulder to collarbone to breast. And when Charlotte's hand slipped between Lily's legs, Lily was ready for her — so ready that as Charlotte entered her, a sound escaped her mouth, the sound a woman can only make at the height of passion — a breathy, desperate . . .

SNORT!

Snort? Lily awoke from her dream to find that her arm was wrapped around not the curvy form of Charlotte, but the flat, hairy chest of Benny Jack McGilly, who was snoring with the volume of a sea lion with bronchitis.

Disoriented and still not quite removed from her dream state, Lily leaped out of bed. Where the hell was she, and what in the name of Sappho was she doing in bed with a man?

SNORT! Ben's snoring shook the bed.

A man with obvious respiratory problems, no less? She backed away from the bed, horrified, only to feel something sharp stick her shoulder blade. She wheeled around to see the black, beady eyes of the stuffed turkey staring at her. She couldn't help it. She screamed.

Ben stopped in mid-snort, sat upright, and flipped on the lamp. "What the — ?"

The peck on the shoulder had woken Lily up. "Um . . . I'm sorry. I was dreaming . . . about Charlotte, and then your snoring woke me up, and I don't know . . . In my dream it was like everything was so normal, and then when I woke up everything was just . . . weird, y'know?"

"Well, that's no excuse for hysteria when some people are trying to sleep. And besides, I do *not* snore."

A knock on the door froze Lily and Ben stiff. "Hey," Big Ben's voice called. "Everything okay in there? We heard screaming."

"Everything's fine, Daddy," Ben said testily. "Go back to bed."

"Oh," Big Ben said. "Oh. Sorry to, uh, interrupt."

Ben's face turned the same shade of red as the preserved turkey's wattle.

"What?" Lily teased. "You're embarrassed that your father thinks you were driving me to screaming heights of ecstasy?"

Ben flipped the light off. "Let's go back to sleep, okay?" He rolled over, and soon the snoring resumed.

Lily crawled back into bed. She hated Ben for waking her up, because she knew that dreams were the only place she'd ever feel Charlotte's touch again. Lily's six years with Charlotte had been a blur of bliss, and now in two short weeks, Lily's life had altered until it was no longer recognizable.

She lay awake, crying softly to herself and praying that Mimi would be safe, until beams of sunlight shot through the bedroom window.

Lily slept just long enough to awake feeling extra groggy. The only thing that'll make you feel worse than not sleeping at all is sleeping just a couple of hours, she thought as she padded stiffly down the hall to check on Mimi. Mimi was in her crib, sleeping with a soundness that Lily envied. She walked down the hall to one of the McGillys' numerous bathrooms.

As she emerged from the shower, she heard Mimi crying. She pulled her clothes on over her damp skin and ran down the hall. By the time she arrived, Mimi was in the throes of a full-blown hysterical fit.

"It's okay, baby. Mama's here." She lifted Mimi out of the crib and hugged her. "You don't like waking up in a strange place any more than your mama does, do you?" She laid her down on one of the bunk beds. "Let's get you out of this pee-pee diaper and see if we can scare you up some breakfast."

Lily carried Mimi downstairs and followed the smell of coffee into the kitchen. "Good morning, Lily!" Jeanie said brightly, dropping two slices of bread into the toaster. "How many eggs can I fix you? Three? Four?"

Eggs first thing in the morning weren't Lily's favorite thing. Her usual breakfast was a piece of fruit washed down with copious amounts of coffee. "One egg is plenty."

Jeanie looked her up and down. "I guess it would be, wouldn't it? You're a tiny little thing. I'm used to feeding boys, and it's a sight how much they eat. When all three of my boys was home, we used to go through six dozen eggs a week." She handed Mimi a sippy cup of milk, Lily a mug of coffee. "Speaking of my boys, I bet that sorry husband of yours ain't turned over in the bed yet."

"He was still pretty out of it when I got up." She sipped from the mug. "Good coffee."

"He always was slow to wake. I used to pour ice water on him to get him outta bed for school." Jeanie set a plate of scrambled eggs and toast in front of Lily. "Hmm," Jeanie said, "I reckon I should just go on and wake him up. I can't just wait around all day to cook his breakfast."

Lily nibbled toast and spooned egg into Mimi's open, baby-bird mouth while Jeanie hollered up the stairs, "Benny Jack! You better get on up! It's going on nine o'clock!"

Lily smiled. Back in Atlanta, Ben rarely rose before eleven.

From upstairs Lily heard Ben yell back a response that sounded like, "oh, for god's sake, Mother." But in two minutes, he was in the kitchen, his face shadowed with stubble and his hair standing on end as if he were a cartoon character who had stuck his finger in a light socket.

"Welcome to married life, Lily," Jeanie said, dropping two more pieces of bread in the toaster. "You might go to bed with a good-looking man, but when he wakes up in the morning, he's gonna look like holy hell."

Lily laughed, while Ben muttered an incantation against the female sex and helped himself to some coffee.

"I'm just teasing you, Benny Jack. You want three eggs or four?"

"Mother, I've told you a thousand times that I don't eat eggs anymore. I know the doctors in Versailles haven't heard of cholesterol yet, but —"

Jeanie rolled her eyes. "I know all about cholesterol, Benny Jack. I just thought you might want a real breakfast this mornin' since it's a special occasion. I mean, if a man don't wake up after his

60

wedding night with a good appetite, then there's somethin' bad wrong —"

"Two," Ben mumbled.

"What was that, honey?"

"Two eggs, Mother." He sank into a kitchen chair.

Mimi pulled herself to standing and leaned against Ben's knee. She grinned up at him with her jack-o'-lantern teeth. "B-Jack," she crooned.

Jeanie looked up from her cooking, delighted. "What was that she said?"

Lily laughed. "I think she just called him Benny Jack."

Jeanie grinned. "Now, Mimi, honey, you don't call him that. You call him daddy, just like always."

Mimi gave Jeanie a puzzled glance. *Daddy* was not a familiar concept to her. She looked back up at Ben, giggled, and repeated, "B-Jack."

Ben slammed down his coffee mug in exasperation. "Ben! Why can't everybody just call me Ben? It's just one little syllable! Is that too much to ask?"

"Now, now, honey," Lily cooed with mock affection. "I think Benny Jack is an *adorable* name." She thought it only fair that if she had to suffer the indignity of being named Lily McGilly, Ben should also be saddled with a name he hated.

Jeanie brought Ben's breakfast to the table. "Your daddy wants y'all to meet him down at the mill at eleven. He's got y'all a one-thirty appointment with Buzz Dobson, but first, he's got a little surprise."

Lily wondered with some trepidation what the surprise could be. Surprises weren't really what she craved these days.

"And I was hoping," Jeanie said, "that you might

leave Mimi with me. I'd just love to show her off and maybe take her shopping. The poor little thing barely has a stitch of clothing to her name."

Lily looked down at Mimi, who was wearing a plain white T-shirt and a pair of tiny denim shorts. Lily had bought most of Mimi's clothes at Goodwill, and her main criteria for selecting infant wear was that it would not be permanently stained by milk, cereal, spit-up, or pee. "I'm sure she would love to go shopping with you," Lily said, against her better instincts.

At five after eleven, Lily and Ben pulled into the gravel parking lot of the Confederate Sock Mill. As they went in the side entrance of the building, with Lily toting Mimi and a bag full of baby supplies, the all-female clerical staff descended on them and crowed, "Oh, is this the new grandbaby?" "I want you to look at her!" "Isn't she the sweetest thing?"

When Jeanie rose from her desk and approached them, the other women cleared a path for her. "There's Mamaw's little sunshine!" she called, opening her arms to receive Mimi. "Benny Jack, your daddy's out on the floor if you want to go get him. You can take Lily, too — show her the production line."

The production area of the Confederate Sock Mill hurt Lily's ears and nose. The clicking and chugging of the machinery was deafening, and the smell of the textile fibers caused her to have a sneezing fit. The two dozen mill workers, engrossed in their repetitive tasks, didn't seem to notice the sounds or smells at all.

Big Ben, who had been deep in conversation with a machine operator, spotted them and waved. "Hey," he yelled over the rumbling machinery. "Y'all ready to go for a ride?"

As they walked to the parking lot, Big Ben said, "Well, I reckon we could go in Benny Jack's car or my truck." He grinned. "Or Lily, we could go in your car."

"Excuse me?"

Big Ben cackled and nodded toward a long, shiny silver car parked in the rear of the lot. "That's for you." He pressed the keys into Lily's hand. "A little wedding present from Jeanie and me."

Lily's vocabulary failed her. "Uh . . . I . . . uh . . ."

"Now I know it ain't as nice as Benny Jack's Lexus," Big Ben apologized. "But you really sprung this marriage thing on us, and a New Yorker was the best we could do on short notice. I tell you what, Lily. You stay married to this rascal a year, and we'll get you any make of car you want!"

"Big Ben, it's a beautiful car, I . . . I just couldn't accept it."

"Of course you can," Big Ben said. "It's just our way of welcoming you into the family. This car's a piece of shit compared to what we got Sheila and Tracee when they married our other boys. But we had a little more notice then, so we could go to Atlanta and pick out somethin' nice, you understand."

"Well, uh . . . thank you." Lily felt as though she were on some bizarre game show, an updated version of *The Liar's Club*, where the gay person who put up the most convincing pretense of heterosexuality could win a snazzy new car.

"So, little lady," Big Ben boomed, "how 'bout taking us for a ride?"

"Sure . . . okay."

The plush interior of the Chrysler New Yorker had that unmistakable new-car smell. It was an undeniably gorgeous vehicle, and yet it wasn't a car Lily would ever have picked out for herself, even if she had possessed the funds to buy it. While she was sure that in Big Ben's eyes, the New Yorker's roominess made it a good family car, to her, a big car meant nothing but bad gas mileage and more exhaust fumes to pollute the environment. Besides, weren't gays supposed to be boycotting the Chrysler company?

Damn it, Lily warned herself, if you're going to pull off the happy hetero bit, you're going to have to start thinking less. She turned the key in the ignition. "Where to?" she asked brightly.

"Hang a left out of the parking lot," Big Ben said from the backseat. He had insisted on sitting in the back so the "newlyweds" could sit in the front together.

Lily hung a left as instructed and drove past barns and fields of cattle. This was her first real experience with country driving, and she had to admit it was much more pleasant than dealing with the stressful, stop-and-go traffic of the city.

"Now turn right at this church over here." Lily turned right at the Free Will Baptist Church — a name which she considered an oxymoron.

"Now you'll wanna go down this road a piece," Big Ben said.

The road was a rural residential area, dotted with well-maintained brick ranch-style houses.

"Now turn at that mailbox that says 104," Big Ben directed.

Lily did as she was told, but had no idea why she was pulling into a strange house's driveway.

She didn't begin to catch on until her hapless husband said, "Now Daddy, what have you gone and done?" At that moment, Lily saw the realty company sign in the yard with the banner across it announcing, SOLD.

"I know it's nothing fancy," Big Ben said, "but it's a good house — built solid — and it'll do ya till you can build the house you really want."

"But, Daddy," Ben said, "we were just going to rent an apartment."

"Now, Benny Jack," Big Ben said, "you know there ain't an apartment in Faulkner County that's worth living in. And besides, you remember that broken-down old trailer you and your mother and me had to live in back when I was first starting the company?"

"No, I don't remember it. We moved out of that trailer when I was two years old."

"Well, it don't matter whether you remember it or not. It was no place to raise a child. And soon as the money from the company started rolling in, I swore that no son of mine would ever have to live without a decent roof over his head." He produced a house key from his jeans pocket. "So whaddaya say, kids? You wanna take a look at her?"

The house had a garage large enough to hold both Ben's Lexus and Lily's new monstrosity of a sedan. Architecturally, the dwelling resembled a brick shoe box. Everything about the house bespoke a normal, heterosexual respectability. Lily hated it.

Inside, the walls were white and the carpeting

65

beige. Each room was square, pristine, and sterile. The only thing Lily liked about it was that there were three bedrooms: one for Mimi, one for Ben, and one for her. "So what kind of monthly payments are we gonna be making on this place?" she asked.

Big Ben looked puzzled. "Payments?"

"Yeah," Lily said. "I mean, you made the down payment, right, but then Ben and I will pay —"

Big Ben hooted. "You and Ben won't have to pay a dime! I bought this house outright — with cash money!"

Lily leaned against a white wall to steady herself. She couldn't imagine having the kind of money where you could just buy a house, any house, on the spot and pay for it all in cash. These people really *were* loaded.

"I know it don't look like much right now, since there ain't a stick of furniture in it," Big Ben said. "But picking out furniture's a woman's job." He checked his watch — a Rolex, Lily noticed. "Lily, if you'd drive us on into town, you'll have plenty of time to pick you out some stuff over at American Home Furnishings before we meet ole Buzz for lunch at the Bucket."

Lily, still leaning against the blank wall, smiled wanly. All her needs were supposedly being taken care of, and yet she had never felt so empty.

Chapter 7

Lily and Ben had just finished a grueling forty-minute shopping spree at American Home Furnishings, during which Lily kept protesting that Big Ben was spending too much money on them, and Ben the younger kept complaining that all the furniture in the store was too tacky to go in any house of his. "It's bad enough," he said, "that I have to live in a ranch-style house. Now I have to furnish it with crap that's just a cut above cardboard!"

"Oh, for godssake." Lily sighed. Her furniture

preference was for antiques and junk-store finds, but if somebody was gracious enough to buy her a houseful of furniture, she wasn't going to be rude enough to complain about the store's limited selection. "Okay," she announced, "we'll take that sea-foam green sofa and armchair and the coffee table that goes with it. We'll also have that round table and chairs over there for the dining room, the oak bedroom suite, the Jenny Lind nursery set, and the maple bedroom suite for the spare room."

The oversolicitous furniture salesman grinned at Ben. "There's something to be said for a lady who knows what she wants."

Every item on the Dinner Bucket's lunch buffet was represented on Buzz Dobson's tie. The fact that he seemed to have trouble conveying a forkful of food to his mouth didn't exactly fill Lily with confidence in his legal abilities. Could a man really have mastered the art of Socratic dialogue if he had never learned how to feed himself?

"So," Lily asked, "where did you go to law school, Mr. Dobson?"

"Oh, call me Buzz," he said, trailing his too-short tie through his mashed potatoes as he reached for his iced tea glass.

"Buzz," Lily corrected herself. While trying not to stare at his gravy-soaked tie, she found herself focusing on Buzz's toupee, a dark brown, vaguely hairlike mass that was perched on his head like a jaunty hat.

"Ahh, I went to law school at your old stomping ground . . . down in Atlanta."

"Emory?" Lily asked, picking at her overcooked macaroni and cheese.

"Naw . . . I went to the Bushrod Washington School of Law . . . it's off of Peachtree."

"Oh, yes, I know it." Under the table, Lily used her index finger to trace the letters *l-o-s-e-r* on Ben's thigh. Spelling out words in this way was a method of communication Dez had invented in order to sit through dull plays and lectures.

Ben traced back on Lily's thigh: *It's okay.*

Lily wasn't sure she believed him. The Bushrod Washington School of Law was housed in a dilapidated, graffiti-sprayed office building. It was widely known as the Last Resort School of Law, an institution whose only entrance requirements were a pulse and a checkbook.

"Yup," Buzz said, discarding a thoroughly gnawed chicken bone, "took me six years, but I finally graduated."

Lily was trying to calculate how quickly she could gather Mimi and her belongings and return to Atlanta when Big Ben said, "Yup, me and Buzz go way back. Ole Buzz was the best running back, Faulkner County High School's ever seen."

Buzz grinned, clearly enjoying the compliment. "You tell that to my poor ole, broke-down knees." He pushed his plate away. Lily expected him to wipe his mouth with his tie, but he didn't. "So," he said, clasping his hands on the table. "I hear you young people are in a spot of trouble. Why don't you tell me a little about it?"

Ben launched into the story he'd concocted, devoting equal detail to the truths, half-truths, and outright lies. When he finished, Buzz turned to Lily. "You got a copy of Charlotte's will on you, honey?"

Lily winced at the unsolicited endearment, but retrieved a photocopy of the will from her bag. Buzz scanned the document, sucking his teeth. "Well," he said finally, "it's all here in black and white, ain't it?" He slipped the document back into its envelope. "Well, first I'm gonna tell you kids what I always tell people. If you got a problem, the best way to settle it is out of court."

Particularly with a lawyer like you, Lily thought, but she kept her lips clamped shut.

"My advice," Buzz continued, "is invite Charlotte's momma and daddy up to Versailles. Have 'em to supper at your new house, or even better, invite 'em over to the big McGilly place — that oughta impress the hell out of 'em. Grill 'em some steaks, let 'em see that Mimi's being taken care of and that y'all are just regular folks like anybody else. My hope is that when they see their granddaughter in a normal, family atmosphere, they'll give up on this foolishness and let you alone."

Lily looked Buzz in the eye. "And if they don't?"

"If they don't, then guess we'll see 'em in court." Buzz glanced over at Big Ben, then looked back at Lily. "Let me put it to you this way, honey. When Big Ben and me played on the same team back in high school, we never lost a game."

* * * * *

"I know what you're thinking, Lily," Big Ben said, as they got into Lily's new ship of a car.

"Really?" She didn't mean to sound snippy, but she still did.

"Uh-huh," Big Ben said, "you're thinking you and Benny Jack woulda fared better if you'd stayed in Atlanta and hired you some hot-shot lawyer."

"Well," Lily admitted, "when I look at Buzz Dobson, *hot shot* isn't exactly a phrase that pops to mind."

Big Ben laughed. "Well, I reckon not. The ole boy can't even hit his mouth with his fork about half the time. But I'll tell you this, Lily. He's a fine feller, and he means well."

Lily pulled out of the parking space and aimed her new tank in the direction of the Confederate Sock Mill. "I'll try to bear that in mind when I lose custody of my daughter."

To her surprise, Big Ben laughed. "She just don't get it, does she, Benny Jack?"

Ben joined his father laughing. "She's a city girl, Daddy. She's not used to how things work in Faulkner County."

"You see, Lily," Big Ben intoned, "it don't matter that Buzz Dobson barely graduated from a fourth-rate law school. We could hire a damn chimpanzee for a lawyer, and we'd still win. We're McGillys, Lily. Me, Benny Jack, you and Mimi, we're all part of the most powerful family in Faulkner County. And besides, me and Judge Sanders play golf together every Wednesday, and half the time I let him win. His son-in-law got himself in a spot of trouble a few years back, and I helped him out of it. People in this county don't forget names nor favors, Lily. There's no way ole Jake Sanders would go against a McGilly."

Lily pulled into the sock mill's gravel parking lot. "I hope you're right."

Big Ben grinned. "Honey, in Faulkner County, I'm always right. I'm a McGilly."

When Ben and Lily walked into the sock mill's office, the clerical workers were abuzz, whispering "here they come" and "won't they be surprised." One of them went to the restroom door and hollered, "Jeanie! They're here!"

"Just a second," Jeanie called from behind the closed door. "We'll be right out."

"What's going on?" Lily asked one of the office workers.

She smiled. "Let's just say that somebody's mamaw took her shopping."

Jeanie opened the door, cooing, "Come on, let's show Mama and Daddy."

Mimi stood in the bathroom doorway, steadying herself against the door facing. She was wearing a cake-frosting-pink dress, the skirt of which was so tiered with stiff, lacy ruffles that the little girl was unable to lay her arms flat at her sides. Instead, she stood with her arms sticking out, like Mr. Potato Head. Her tiny feet were encased in stiff white patent-leather Mary Janes, and a lacy headband with a pink bow clued in anyone who might not yet have picked up on the fact that this was indeed a female child.

"So, what do you think?" Jeanie asked, beaming.

Lily started laughing — a more socially acceptable reaction than crying, which had been her other impulse. "She's . . . she's . . . a sight." Mimi looked mad

72

as hell, just like Charlotte used to look when she had to wear a dress and high heels.

"Good god, Mother, how much did you pay for all that crap?" Ben asked.

"Now, Benny Jack, don't you say a word. A mamaw's got to splurge on her only granddaughter a little bit. We just went over to the Little Princess shop in Callahan, and then after that we stopped at McDonald's for a Happy Meal." Jeanie scooped Mimi up in her arms. "And Lord, you shoulda seen this girl put away them Chicken McNuggets!"

"She's . . . she's never eaten meat before." Lily had pledged to raise Mimi a vegetarian, at least until she got old enough to make her own dietary decisions.

"Well, I'll tell you what," Jeanie said. "She eat them Chicken McNuggets like she was going to the chair."

It was so easy, Lily thought, to plan how you would raise your child — to say with absolute certainty the things you would and would not do. But once the child got exposed to outside influences, all those plans were shot to hell. "Well . . . Mimi, I guess we'd better get you home for your nap. You've had quite a day." She picked her daughter up. Her new dress must have added five pounds to her weight. Or maybe it was the Chicken McNuggets. "Thank you, Jeanie, for taking her shopping and . . . taking care of her."

As they walked out of the building, Ben said, "You look like you've been poleaxed."

"I'm just overwhelmed. The house, the car . . ." When she set Mimi in her car seat, Mimi's lacy petticoat flew up high enough to obscure her little face. "And Mimi . . . god . . . leave her with your mother for two hours and . . ."

"She becomes a meat-eating femme fatale?"

Lily's laugh gave way to an uneasy sigh. She leaned against the car. "Maybe having the Maycombs over for dinner will work things out. I just want this whole custody thing taken care of as soon as possible. It's scary how fast stuff can change your life, y'know?" She wiped away a stray tear, missing Charlotte.

"I know." Ben gave her a little pat before he headed to his car. "I'll see you back at the house, okay?"

"Okay."

Lily slid into the driver's seat. "So Mimi-saurus," she said, "how 'bout we go back to the house and take a nap?"

"No nap!" Mimi screamed from her car seat. "Go McDonald's!"

Chapter 8

When Ben, Lily, and Mimi returned to the big McGilly house, a huge black animal was sprawled on the porch. "Oh, shit," Ben swore. "Mordecai's gotten out of his pen again."

"Excuse me?" Lily said.

"The dog. Mother and Daddy've been keeping him in the pen out back since we got here. They were afraid he'd scare Mimi."

Lily paused before opening the car door. "Is he dangerous?"

"He was when he was younger, but now he's just old and cantankerous. He sleeps and farts most of the time. He's always been good with kids, though, and if you call him by his name, he knows you're friendly and won't bother you."

Just to be safe, Lily carried Mimi extra high on her hip when they reached the porch.

"Mordecai!" Ben called when they approached the door.

The rottweiler raised his huge head, glanced at Ben, and lowered it again.

"Cow!" Mimi exclaimed delightedly.

"He's a doggie, sweetie," Lily corrected her, "but he's just about big enough to be a cow. His name's Mordecai."

At the sound of his name, Mordecai looked up at Lily and wagged his stumpy tail.

"Wow," Ben said, unlocking the front door, "that's the most energy I've seen him expend in years."

When they walked into the house, Mordecai followed Lily close behind. At the stairs she said, "You wait here, Mordecai. I'm gonna put Mimi down for her nap."

When Lily came back downstairs, Mordecai was still sitting there dutifully. When she sat on the living room sofa, he joined her there, his bulky body occupying the length of the sofa, his huge head in Lily's lap.

"That's amazing," Ben said. "I've never seen him act that way around anybody."

"Well," Lily said, stroking Mordecai's huge head. "I'm afraid he scores more points than you do in the doting-husband category." She sighed at the thought of having to contact the Maycombs. "But if you want to improve your score, you can hand me the phone. I believe we have a dinner invitation to proffer."

Lily dialed the Maycombs' number and waited nervously for an answer. After three rings, Charlotte's mother trilled a melodic "Hello."

Shit, Lily thought, before she dialed, she should have figured out what she was going to say. "Um, hi, Mrs. Maycomb? This is Lily."

"Lily Fox?"

How many Lilys do you know, old woman? she thought, but she said sweetly, "Yes, although that's not my last name anymore. I . . . married recently."

"Married?" Ida Maycomb squawked like a mynah. "To a man?"

Well, sort of. "Why, yes, of course. I'm Mrs. Ben McGilly now," Lily said, gagging slightly. "The thing is . . . Ben, Mimi, and I are living up in Versailles now, and his family and I wanted to invite you to dinner some night. You could spend some time with Mimi, meet her other grandparents . . . and we could talk. I know we've had our differences in the past, and I was hoping we could sit down to a meal together and maybe straighten things out."

"Well . . . um, I don't know, Lily." Ida's voice quivered with the uneasiness of a person who never makes her own decisions. "I'd have to ask Charles, of course. And Mike . . . would he be invited?"

"Sure," Lily said cheerily, even as her stomach lurched at the thought of this horrid gathering.

"And when would this dinner be?"

"How about Saturday at six? Ben can meet you at the interstate exit to show you the way to the house." Ben glowered at her, and she stuck out her tongue at him.

"Well . . ." Ida waffled. "I'll tell you what. I'll talk to Charles when he gets home and see what he says."

"Okay, well, let me give you the number here." Ida hung up the second Lily recited the last digit.

Two beers for Lily and three dog biscuits for Mordecai later, the phone rang. Lily had only gone so far as to say "Hel —" when Ida said, "We'll be there — Saturday at six." Click.

"Well, they're coming," Lily sighed.

Ben shook his head. "It's kinda hard to figure out whether that's good news or not, isn't it?"

That night, Mordecai slept in the bed between Lily and Ben, taking up more than his fair share of room. Between Ben's snores and Mordecai's flatulence, Lily could scarcely sleep for the noise and air pollution. Soon, she comforted herself, they'd be in their shoe box of a house, where at least they could sleep in canine-free separate beds.

The housekeeper had dusted, scoured, or vacuumed every available surface of the McGillys' colonial–antebellum–style home. In thirty minutes, Ben would be meeting the Maycombs at the Versailles interstate exit to escort them to the house. Right now, though, Lily and Ben sat on opposite ends of the slate-blue and mauve living room, dreading the evening ahead of them.

Jeanie strode into the room, nervously glancing at her gold watch. "Benny Jack, you heard me tell your daddy to be home by five-fifteen so he could change into some decent clothes, didn't you?"

"Yes, Mother, I heard you."

"Well, if you heard me, why the hell didn't he?" Jeanie was wearing a peach jersey sundress and tan canvas espadrilles. A small strand of undoubtedly real pearls hung just below the hollow of her throat. Her curly brown hair hung loose around her tanned shoulders. She looked stylish, comfortable, and very, very rich.

Lily was wearing a sky-blue dress she had borrowed from Jeanie. Except for her most faded pair of Levi's, it was the lightest-colored garment she had worn since she was a kid. But for Mimi she'd suffer anything — even pastels.

Lily looked down at her daughter, who was playing on the floor and wearing a mint-green smocked dress. Lily watched as Mimi spotted Mordecai, a demonic gleam in her eye. "Mookie!" she squealed, then pulled herself to standing at the coffee table, walked three tentative steps, and fell smack on her diaper-padded butt.

"Omigod!" Lily yelled at the exact same moment Jeanie did. Lily picked Mimi up and swung her through the air. "Mimi-saurus, that was great! You're a toddler now!"

"Did you see that, Benny Jack?" Jeanie was breathless with excitement. "Your little girl just took her first steps!"

"Yeah," Ben said, sounding completely devoid of interest. "Well, I guess I'd better go pick up the Cobb County cretins now."

As he headed out the door, Jeanie shook her head in exasperation. "Men. Sometimes I think they just don't know what's important in life." She turned her attention to Mimi. "Now, I think a big walking girl ought to at least get a cookie if her mama says it's okay."

Lily smiled. "Of course it's okay. This is a special occasion."

Jeanie and Lily assembled a salad while Mimi nibbled her cookie. "It would be great if Mimi would walk in front of the Maycombs tonight," Lily said, slicing a cucumber that she was secretly thinking of as Mike Maycomb's penis. "That way, they'd see she's developing normally in this environment —"

"You know," Jeanie said, chopping a tomato, "Big Ben told me about Mimi not being yours by blood, but I've never seen nobody love a child the way you love her. If these people can't see that, there's something bad wrong with them."

Lily felt her eyes fill, and it was carrot, not onion, that she was chopping. "Mimi's the world to me. She's all I've got."

"Besides Benny Jack, you mean?"

"Yeah, right. Besides Benny Jack."

Just as Jeanie had feared, Ida, Charles, and Mike Maycomb arrived at the house before Big Ben. Big Ben's absence made Lily nervous. She knew the Maycombs would be more comfortable if there was a patriarch presiding over the evening's events, and as far as patriarchs went, Ben the younger didn't quite fit the bill.

When Ben the younger walked in with Ida, Charles, and Mike, a rictus of a smile was frozen on his face — the kind of grin worn by a death's head. "Come on in," he said, through clenched teeth. "Lily and I would've invited you over to our new place, but you would've had to sit on unpacked boxes."

The three Maycombs glanced around the living room — approvingly, Lily hoped. Despite the hot weather, Charles and Ida were both dressed for a Sunday service at Calvary Baptist. They looked as starched and proper as Dick and Pat Nixon in their heyday. Mike, however, was going for a more casual look. In his ridiculous fuchsia polo shirt with matching fuchsia and kelly green plaid pants, he was dressed for a day on the golf course.

Ida nodded at Lily and emitted a frosty "Hello."

"Hi," Lily said as brightly as she could manage. "I'm glad y'all could make it."

Ida's frostiness melted away when her eyes came to rest on Mimi. "There she is!" she whooped. "Grandma's little precious!"

Mimi stretched out her arms. "Gamma!" Ida picked up her granddaughter and held her close.

"She took her first steps today," Lily said.

"She did?" Ida crooned, "Gwamma's little angel's getting to be a big girl. Charles, did you hear that?"

"Sure did." Charles shifted his feet uncomfortably, obviously wishing he was in a setting where he would feel more comfortable, like a book burning or a Klan rally. He looked over at Mike for a cue. Lily had noticed how both Ida and Charles tended to follow Mike's lead. To them, their son was one of the greatest minds of this, or any, century. Lily had no doubt that contesting her custody of Mimi had been Mike's big idea . . . and that he had convinced Ida and Charles of its wisdom.

"Hel-lo!" Jeanie half sang, emerging from the kitchen as though she was making her big entrance in a play. "Please, sit down, and make yourselves at home. I'm Jeanie McGilly, Ben's mama." She shook hands with her guests, who introduced themselves. "I am so sorry that my husband hasn't arrived yet. I'm sure you know how hard it is to drag a man away from work, don't you, Ida?" Jeanie's smile was stunning. "Can I get you folks anything to drink before dinner?"

Lily saw Charles recoil slightly. The Maycombs were teetotalers who regarded anyone who drank so much as a beer a day as a hopeless alcoholic. Jeanie must have noticed Charles's reaction, too, because she added, "Iced tea? Lemonade?"

They all sat in the living room, glasses of lemonade in hand, unable to come up with a single topic of conversation. Lily sat close to Ben on the couch, her hand in his. It was difficult to pretend to be in love. Real love was such a natural flow of feeling that it was hard to know how to fake it.

"So, Lily," Ida said at the point where the sipping of lemonade was becoming a deafening sound, "how did you and Ben meet?"

"Oh, we've been friends for years," Lily said, trying to smile at Ben adoringly. "It was only recently that we started to become . . . more." She attempted a giggle, but stopped it when she decided she sounded demented.

"Yeah," Ben added, "Lily and me together — who'd have thought it?"

"It's just like that movie *When Harry Met Sally*," Jeanie said, "where the couple's been friends for years before they realize they were meant to be together. I just love mushy movies like that, don't you, Ida?"

"We don't see many movies," Charles answered for her. "Too much bad language."

Jeanie smiled politely. "It is a sight, isn't it?"

"Well, I think we all know who's in charge of Hollywood," Mike said. "And it's not the Christians."

Lily squeezed Ben's hand so hard she expected to hear the bones crack. They had been sitting in uncomfortable silence for a few moments when the front door swung open. "Oh, that must be my husband," Jeanie said.

It was. Big Ben was wearing his customary plain white T-shirt, blue jeans, and work boots, but he was smeared from head to toe with what appeared to be axle grease. His lips looked startlingly pink in contrast to the black gunk on his face. "One of the blame machines at the mill broke down, and I had to fix it. You want something done right, you gotta do it yourself." He nodded at the Maycombs. "I'm Benny Jack's daddy, by the way. Ever'body calls me Big Ben." He looked down at his grease-blackened paw. "Don't mean to seem standoffish, but I don't reckon y'all'd wanna be shaking my hand right now."

"Honey —" Jeanie's voice was tense. "Why don't you take a shower before you put the steaks on?"

"I reckon I will." Big Ben wiped his brow, smearing grease across his forehead. "Think I'll just grab me a be — a Co'Cola first." It was Big Ben's custom to consume a six-pack of Budweiser between the time he got home from work and the time he went to bed, but Lily had asked him to abstain while in the Maycombs' presence.

Later, as they sat around the dining room table, everyone but Lily and Mimi slicing into huge, bloody slabs of steak, Ida chirped, "Lily, I just don't see how you can stand to be a vegetarian. I mean, what do you *eat*?"

Lily smiled so tensely that her jaws ached. "Everything but meat." She speared a forkful of salad.

"Well," Charles began, "doesn't it say in the Bible, though, that the Lord gave man dominion over animals?"

"Well, Lily's softhearted when it comes to animals," Ben said. "You know how women are."

Charles, Ben, Mike, and Big Ben all shared a laugh about the sentimentality of womenfolk. While wringing her napkin under the table as though it were a human neck, Lily noticed that Jeanie rolled her eyes at the men, while Ida laughed right along with them.

They were very different women, Jeanie and Ida. While Jeanie might enjoy reading a romance novel while lounging in the pool, she definitely knew the difference between fantasy and reality. She never let a man have the final word just because of his gender, and as a mother and a businesswoman, she exuded competence and confidence.

Ida, however, lived in a world in which she unquestioningly took orders from God and her husband, not necessarily in that order. No matter what her husband and son said, she smiled in agreement. If Ida ever had any complaints, Lily was sure that she muttered them under her breath instead of saying them out loud.

"You know," Charles began, "I was just saying when we were driving through Versailles how I kinda envy y'all for living in this small town. Some of the best folks anywhere live in small-town America — God-fearing, hardworking people who aren't afraid to do for each other."

Or to mind each other's business, Lily thought.

"Don't get me wrong," Charles continued, "I like where we live out in Cobb County. I could never live right in Atlanta, though. There's a certain element there I just don't want to associate with. I think you know who I mean: the crack dealers, the prostitutes, just all the bla —"

"People who haven't found Jesus yet," Mike finished for him.

Of course, Lily thought. You Lieutenants of the Lord are willing to disguise your racism in order to preserve the patriarchy.

"Well, of course," Ida said, smiling sweetly, "there are . . . undesirables wherever you go. In small towns, you get the trailer trash and the Holy Rollers."

"How's that?" Big Ben asked, leaning over the table intently.

"What my wife means is, those Church of God people," Charles said. "You know, the ones that shout and dance and speak in tongues and act crazy."

"They're very unrefined," Ida said, with a superior simper.

"Some of 'em even drink strychnine and set themselves on fire," Mike laughed.

Big Ben set down his knife and fork. "I was raised in the Church of God. Now, we wasn't the kind to handle snakes or set ourselves afire or nothin' like that. But we would shout and speak in tongues and get happy. And you wanna talk about some fine people . . . they was some of the best folks you'd ever meet in that church." He took a slug of Coke. "Now, I ain't in that church no more, mind you. Jeanie and Mama joined up with the Presbyterians a while back, and I joined up with 'em. I don't hardly go to church there, though, 'cause the preaching and the singing's so quiet, it seems like I have to start snoring just to make a little noise.

"I'll tell you somethin', though. A few years back I was down in Mississippi on bizness, and I looked up this ole army buddy of mine — a black feller. He invited me to a tent revival his church was having. I was the only white man in that tent, and I swear to God, I don't believe I sat down once during the whole service . . . I was too busy standing up and clapping and singing. Them people knew how to have church, let me tell you." Big Ben picked up his silverware and dug back into his steak.

"Well, of course, there's good people in every group," Charles waffled. "I didn't mean —"

"I know what you meant, buddy," Big Ben said, looking Charles in the eye.

"So," Jeanie said, with determined cheer. "We got pound cake and chess pie. Who wants what?"

As everyone sat with their coffee in the living room, Lily crawled down on the floor with Mimi and helped her to a standing position. "How about a little after-dinner entertainment, Mimi-saurus?" Lily said. "Why don't you show Grandma and Grandpa how you can walk?"

Mimi stood with her little hands clenched, steeling herself for action.

"Come on, sweetie. Walk to Mama."

Mimi knitted her brow, sucked in her breath, and

took one, two, three faltering steps before falling into Lily's arms. At the sound of her grandparents' applause, she grinned crookedly.

"I swear," Big Ben said, "I think she's just about the happiest baby I've ever seen."

"Well, of course she's happy," Jeanie added. "Why wouldn't she be? She's well taken care of, and loved." She looked straight at the Maycombs. "Mimi may not be hers by blood, but Lily's still one of the best mamas I've ever seen."

Lily's stomach clenched. All evening she had been wondering how to broach the subject of Mimi's custody with the Maycombs. Now it seemed that Big Ben and Jeanie were going to cut to the chase for her, which, she noticed, had caused the Maycombs to squirm as though the cushions in their chairs were stuffed with gravel.

"Well," Charles said, avoiding eye contact with anyone in the room. "I'm sure Lily is fine at seeing to the child's basic needs — keeping her fed and clean, that kind of thing." He smiled self-righteously. "But as I'm sure some of the ladies in the room know, there's a lot more to being a mother than that."

"Oh, yes." Ida looked at Mike in the same way Jocasta must have looked at Oedipus. "If you've not carried the child in your own body, you don't know what it is to be a mother. Nobody knows children like a real mother does."

That's funny, Lily thought. You barely could have picked your daughter out of a lineup.

"Well, that's certainly a sentiment you could needlepoint on a pillow," Ben said. "But Mimi's

87

biological mother is no longer with us. Lily and I are just trying to create the best family for her that we can."

"Well," Charles said calmly, "we feel that Mimi needs to be in an environment where she can learn the difference between right and wrong —"

"Now you just hold on a minute here," Big Ben interrupted. "You can ask anybody in Faulkner County, and they'll tell you the McGillys is fine folks. We're a decent, hardworking family, and Benny Jack here is a good boy. We never had a bit of trouble outta him, and I can't say the same thing for his brothers. And Lily — she may not look like you're used to girls looking, but she's a good, honest person."

The word *honest* stung Lily, but she was touched by Big Ben's impassioned defense.

"Look," Mike said impatiently, "there are certain factors here you don't understand. I don't want to go into them because there are ladies present. Let's just say that given these factors, we feel it would be in Mimi's best interests to live with the remaining members of her biological family."

"But Mike," Lily interjected, "Ben is Mimi's biological father." So much for the honesty theory, she thought.

"Oh, I don't believe that story for a minute. Mimi's daddy was in some test tube at a sperm bank." Mike's bald spot flushed red, and a vein in his forehead bulged. "Just because you found some sissy to marry you, just because you put on a dress and shaved your legs, that doesn't change what you are —"

"Calm down, son —" Charles interrupted.

Heedless, Mike ranted on. "And don't think for a second we don't know who you are, Lily . . . *McGilly*, as you call yourself. For whatever perverted purposes, you may claim to be a normal wife and mother, but deep down you're still a godless, man-hating —"

A crash issued from upstairs as though a door had been ripped from its sockets. Something huge barreled down the stairs and soon was standing on its hind legs with its front paws positioned on the arms of Mike's chair. A low growl issued from its black, curled-back lips.

"Mordecai!" Big Ben hollered. "Down, boy!"

The rottweiler didn't budge. Mike's face, so recently aflame with anger, was now frozen in terror.

"Mordecai!" Lily called. "Down, boy."

Mordecai wagged his stump of a tail at Lily and moved his bulk to rest in front of her and Mimi, creating a physical barrier between them and the Maycombs.

"Oh, I see how it is." Mike rose from his chair. His plaid pants looked suspiciously damp to Lily. "You invite us down here so you can make a mockery of us. You sic your dog on us —"

"Now hold on a minute, buddy," Big Ben interrupted. "We didn't sic our dog on you. He was shut in the bedroom upstairs."

"He musta heard you yelling at Lily," Jeanie said. "Ever since Lily got here, Mordecai's just took to her. It's like he's her protector —"

"My knight in shining flea collar," Lily said, hoping a joke would lighten the bleak situation. It didn't.

"Well . . ." Ida was holding her purse in her lap. "It's getting awfully late." She looked at Charles hopefully.

He picked up his cue. "Yes, it is, and we've got a long drive ahead of us. Thank you for dinner —"

"Wait," Ben said. Everyone's head turned toward him. "My wife and I asked you here tonight in hopes that we could settle our differences outside a courtroom. Now, Lily and I have talked about this a lot, and we both agree that you can see Mimi as often as you like — as long as you agree to respect the terms of Charlotte's will."

"I loved my daughter," Charles began. "But no matter what my feelings for Charlotte were, I can't uphold her will. We . . . just feel that Charlotte was under some . . . undesirable influences" — Lily felt Charles's disapproving stare. " — when she wrote the will. And it was bad enough for those influences to affect my daughter. There's no way I'm going to let them affect my granddaughter!"

Lily was seething. They always made it sound as though Lily had converted Charlotte . . . corrupted her into leading an "undesirable" lifestyle. Charlotte had known she was a dyke since she was twelve years old! "Charlotte was a grown woman —"

"I think what Daddy is saying," Mike interrupted as he headed for the door, "is that we already have a lawyer. Maybe you should think of hiring one, too."

"Oh, don't you worry about that, funny boy." Big Ben was making no effort to hide his anger. "We've got us a lawyer. We was hoping we wouldn't have to use him, but there's just no talking to some people. I believe you can find your way back to the interstate exit. And I reckon the next time we'll see you will be in the Faulkner County Courthouse."

Mike glowered at Big Ben. "Fine. This seems like a decent town. I'm sure they'll do the right thing."

Big Ben grinned. "I'm sure they will, too. Don't let the door hit your ass on the way out, now."

After the Maycombs' car had backed out of the driveway, Big Ben said, "Okay, who wants a beer now that the Baptists is gone?"

Everybody but Mimi raised a hand.

Chapter 9

"Ganny!" Mimi squealed when Lily opened the front door for Granny McGilly, who was weighed down with a heavy-looking cardboard box.

"Here, let me take that for you," Lily said, relieving the old woman of the box's weight.

"That's just a few little ole things I thought you could use to brighten the place up a little ... a picture or two, a few little gewgaws. I'm getting to the age where little things like that just look like clutter to me. I thought maybe you could use 'em."

"Well, thank you." Lily looked at the framed

picture that was sticking up out of the box: a Victorian print of a golden-haired female angel guiding two dimple-faced children across a bridge. It was kitschy, but Lily kind of liked it. "Nice picture."

"That pitcher'd been hanging in my bedroom for years, but yesterday, I got to looking at it, and it put me in mind of Mimi — in all this trouble you're having, it seems like she needs her a guardian angel."

Lily was touched. Since the disastrous dinner with the Maycombs, all the McGilly clan had rallied around Lily, telling her those awful people had no right to treat her that way and that they'd live to regret the day they crossed a McGilly. Their support made Lily feel reassured and guilty at the same time — guilty because she knew the McGillys would feel differently if they found out her and Ben's marriage was a fraud.

"Mimi definitely needs all the help she can get," Lily said. "Buzz Dobson's working on setting up a date for the hearing. I'm a nervous wreck about the whole thing."

"Don't you worry," Granny McGilly said. "There ain't never been a McGilly to lose in court in this county." She nodded toward the door. "I got somethin' else for you out in the truck, but I don't know how excited you'll be to see it."

Lily picked up Mimi and followed Granny outside. There, in the bed of the green Chevy truck, was Mordecai, panting and wagging his stump of a tail.

"Mookie!" Mimi exclaimed.

"Uh . . . what's Mordecai doing here?" Lily asked. It was a question she feared she already knew the answer to.

"Well, I stopped by the big house on the way over here. Jeanie said that ever since you moved out,

Mordecai's stayed up all night howling for you. He won't eat, neither. Just sleeps all day and howls all night. Big Ben said he reckoned if Mordecai loved you that much, he orta go live with you. He's too old to be much of a guard dog anyway."

Lily looked into the big dog's adoring, chocolate-brown eyes. "Well, I don't know what Ben will think of this —"

"Benny Jack's mother and daddy write him a check for five thousand dollars every month even though he don't do a lick of work for the company. I figure five thousand a month's enough to cover the care and feeding of a dog."

"Well, I guess it is," Lily said. "Come on, Mordecai. The backyard's fenced in. I guess we can put you out there for the time being."

Mordecai jumped out of the bed of the truck, delighted.

"So, Mimi," Lily asked, "do you want Mordecai to be your doggie?"

Mimi wrapped her arms around Mordecai's bull neck and cooed, "Big doggie. *My* doggie."

Well, they were cute together. Lily didn't know how she and Mimi would handle having such a big dog when they moved back to the city, but then a terrifying but familiar image flashed in her mind: She might not have Mimi when she moved back to the city.

"You okay, honey?" Granny McGilly asked.

"Yeah . . . just kinda stressed out."

Granny patted her shoulder. "You're a high-strung little thing, ain'tcha? I told you not to worry about nothin'. This ugliness in court'll be settled soon enough, and then you and Benny Jack can get back to being a normal married couple."

A normal married couple. Yeah, right. Lily watched Granny climb into her truck and drive off, noticing for the first time the rifle in the gun rack of the truck's back window. Lily had no trouble picturing Granny using that gun, firing away at squirrels or rabbits or the Maycombs. Now, that last image was one she could enjoy.

That afternoon, Ben came in the door, humming. When Mimi announced his presence with a squeal of "B-Jack," instead of correcting her, he picked her up and swung her like an airplane.

"B-Jack funny," Mimi laughed.

Ben smiled the kind of smile someone in a Walt Disney cartoon might when a bluebird alights on his shoulder. "B-Jack certainly is." He focused for a second on the guardian angel picture Lily had just finished hanging over the couch. "Say, isn't that picture from Granny's house?"

"Yeah, she brought it over this morning. She brought something else, too, which might not make you too happy."

"Mordecai? Yeah, I saw him as I drove up. That's okay. He's not so bad, as quadrupeds go."

Lily looked at Ben in amazement. "So . . . what happened to that adorable, perpetually kvetching homosexual that I married?"

Ben sat down in the armchair, hugging his knees. "I had a good day, that's all."

"Do tell. It's the first good day you've had since we moved to Versailles, so I think that makes it a newsworthy event."

"Well, this morning when I was dropping those papers off at Buzz Dobson's office, I kind of ran into somebody from my past."

"Your past?" Lily teased. "I didn't know you had a past."

"F-u-c-k y-o-u," Ben said, spelling his profanity so Mimi wouldn't parrot it. "It was this guy, Ken, I went to high school with. And god, I was obsessed with him back then . . . he was a nerdy little gay boy's wet dream: a National Merit Scholar, president of the Beta Club, and with these big, brown eyes to die for. Have you ever known anybody like that? Somebody you just can't stop thinking about?"

"Just Charlotte. I don't think I'll ever be able to go five minutes without thinking of her." She shook off her pain. "Sorry. Didn't mean to get maudlin. So you ran into this guy today?"

"Sure did. Now he's a chemistry professor over at Faulkner County Community College. I was kind of surprised that he's teaching there, but the academic market's tough these days. He's still gorgeous, and . . ." Ben paused dramatically. "He's never married."

"So do you think —"

"I think he might be. I mean, he dated girls in high school, but hell, *I* even dated a girl or two in high school. He really set my gaydar off today, but it could just be wishful thinking."

"Shame on you!" Lily laughed. "A married man!"

Ben flashed another Walt Disney grin. "On

Saturday, he and I are playing golf at the country club."

Lily felt a sudden tingle of fear. "Now, Ben, you have to be discreet about this —"

"Do you honestly think there's anybody in this town who would think of two men — one of them married — playing golf together at the country club as a *date*?"

"No, I guess not. Excuse my paranoia — it's just that I know for a fact that there are people out to get me."

"I promise to be discreet. Hell, there's probably not even going to be anything to be discreet about. I don't even know if this is a date." He tried to fight the smile creeping across his lips. "But I hope it is."

Chapter 10

Lily was trying to work. She sat at the kitchen table, with a spiral notebook and a sketch pad in front of her. When she was starting a new children's book, she never knew which would come to her first: the words or the pictures. She rested her chin in her hands and stared into space. She rubbed Mordecai, who was resting under the table, with her bare feet.

Today, neither the words nor the pictures were coming.

But it wasn't just that she was having an off day. Since the accident, since the Maycombs' attack, Lily hadn't made a single sketch or written anything more creative than a grocery list. Her hands, which in happier days had itched with the urge to create, were now numb and impotent.

The problem with being an artist, Lily thought, is that my work reflects my life. During her days with Charlotte, Lily's happiness had spilled forth onto the pages of her books. Her playful spirit had perfectly matched the spirits of her young readers.

Now, though, her spirit was far from happy and playful, and she refused to write a children's book that reflected her current state of mind. Lily couldn't write a children's book about the all-too-human capacity for inhumanity, oppression, and injustice. Children would learn about these things soon enough without reading a book about them.

And Mimi, who was now napping so innocently in her crib, might learn about these things all too soon. She might be taken away from the person who loved her most in the world by the people who thought that person wasn't fit to live. Lily rested her head in her hands. She tried to take comfort in the McGillys' confidence in the hearing's outcome, but it was confidence she couldn't share. The McGillys' lack of concern concerned her.

Mordecai hefted his bulk up and ambled toward the kitchen door.

"Need to go out, tiny boy?" Lily called Mordecai by diminutive names, like "teensy lapdog" and "my little Chihuahua." The one-hundred-eighty-pound beast seemed to enjoy thinking of himself as a daintier creature.

Once Mordecai was in the backyard, she closed her notebook and her sketch pad. If the inspiration isn't there, she had learned, there's no forcing it. Still, she was going to have to get some inspiration from somewhere. Regardless of how the trial went, there would be a day in the not-so-distant future when she would be kicked off the McGilly family gravy train.

She used her once-creative hands to make tea and wash dishes. What a fine little housewife I'm turning out to be, she thought.

Ben, of course, was out with his new/old obsession. The golfing date had gone well; Ben had come home so excited about spending the day with Ken that Lily had suggested that he change his name to Barbie. "Besides," she had said, "you don't really want to go through life as a couple named Ben and Ken."

"Is it any more ridiculous than going through life as Lily McGilly?"

Lily had conceded his point. She also had to concede something else: Her sarcasm toward Ben's giddiness was due to nothing more than good, old-fashioned jealousy. It didn't bother her that her ersatz husband was stepping out on her; she didn't give a shit about that.

It was Ben's happiness that drove her crazy, that made her think of her first days with Charlotte, when their love was green and about to blossom. That kind of joy was the complete opposite of what she was feeling these days. Tennyson may have believed that " 'Tis better to have loved and lost than never to have loved at all," but Lily wasn't sure.

Of course, there wasn't anything for Lily to be jealous of yet. Neither Ben nor Ken had admitted to the other that he was gay. Ben said they had each "dropped a few hairpins" during their game of golf, but being in a public place, neither of them had let his hair down entirely.

Today, though, they were meeting in a more private setting. Ken had invited Ben to spend the afternoon at his house, listening to Brit pop and then eating sushi for dinner, which Ken had prepared from ingredients he had bought at the international farmer's market in Atlanta. Lily had opined to Ben that he was home free: straight white men don't make sushi.

Lily dried the last dish and sipped her tea. Just then, her eardrums were pierced by a high-pitched cry of pain. She dropped her cup into the sink and ran to Mimi's room, only to find the little girl resting comfortably. She heard the cry again, and this time, with her maternal instinct laid to rest, she could tell the sound was animal, not human. It was coming from the backyard.

She ran down the hall and out the kitchen door. Mordecai was lying on his stomach, his face pressed against the chain-link fence, whimpering and howling in pain.

"It's okay, Mordecai," she said as she approached him. "It's me, Mordecai." Animals in pain, she knew, could strike out without thinking. She softly repeated his name to remind him that she was his friend.

When she got closer, she saw what had happened. Mordecai, famous for digging his way out of his dog pen at the big McGilly house, had attempted to do the same thing with the chain-link fence here. But he had hit a painful snag.

The section of fencing he had exposed was torn, as though someone had clipped a jagged hole in it — a hole just the right size to trap one of his mammoth front paws.

There was a lot of blood. In trying to remove his paw from the trap, he had only succeeded in digging the metal into his flesh.

"Poor baby," Lily cooed. Mordecai whimpered in agreement.

Lily locked her fingers in the links above the hole and pulled upward. The big dog looked down at his freed paw with mournful eyes.

Lily had to agree that it did look pretty bad. His dark fur made the nature of his wounds hard to detect, but when he tried to stand, the injured foot dangled limply. For all Lily knew, it could be broken.

"Sit tight, Mordecai. Let me go inside and get the baby and the car keys. We're gonna get you some help."

The one thing she could say in favor of the monstrous Chrysler New Yorker Big Ben had bought was that it was a vehicle of sufficient size to comfortably transport a toddler and a rottweiler. Lily's old Honda, which was sitting unused in the condo parking lot in Atlanta, barely had enough room for her and Mimi, let alone a one-hundred-eighty-pound dog. She had wrapped Mordecai's paw in a clean towel. Even so, she was sure he was bleeding all over the car's plush upholstery. She knew this kind of thing would cause Ben to have a hissy fit, but she didn't care. The day she cared more about personal property than living things was the day she'd have her woman's symbol tattoo removed and become a cheeseburger-chomping Republican.

After Lily was already on the road, it occurred to her that she could have called Jeanie and asked who

Mordecai's regular vet was. But it was too late for that. Since he was losing blood, expediency seemed the best path. Down the road from the sock mill, she had noticed a green double-wide trailer with a sign, FAULKNER COUNTY ANIMAL CLINIC. Lily hoped they would see animals on an emergency basis.

Once they arrived, Lily had no doubt that the Faulkner County Animal Clinic was where Mordecai went for his shots and checkups. He had been exceptionally cooperative about getting into the car at the house, but now, at the sight of the foreboding trailer, he froze in terror. Being careful to avoid his hurt foot, Mimi tried to pull him out of the car, but it was impossible. His huge muscles were locked, such that moving him was as impossible as moving a heavy marble statue.

"Okay, fine. You wait here." She left the window cracked for the obstinate canine and freed Mimi from her car seat. Mimi grabbed her hand and toddled alongside her to the trailer's entrance.

A round old lady with a pink slash of lipstick on her puckered mouth sat at the desk in the paneled waiting room. "May I help you, dear?" she asked, through puckered lips.

"Um, yes, I hope so," Lily said. "I don't have an appointment, but I have an injured dog in the car. He's Big Ben McGilly's —"

"Mordecai?" the old lady asked.

Lily was amazed. She had already discovered that every person knew every other person in this town, but until now, she hadn't realized that this knowledge extended to lower members of the animal kingdom. "Yes, that's him."

"Well, you can bring him on in."

"Well, actually, I can't. He won't budge from the car."

The old lady smiled. "Well, I guess if Mordecai doesn't want to move, it's kinda hard to make him. Have a seat. I'll get Dr. Jack to help you."

Lily sat down on a green vinyl chair. Mimi stood at the waiting room's coffee table, clearly fascinated by the lamp that sat on it. A ginger-jar lamp, its clear glass base was filled with dog biscuits.

The old lady, who had disappeared into the back of the trailer, returned to her post at the desk. "The doctor'll be with you in a minute."

Moments later, Lily looked up as she heard the sound of boots clomping down the linoleum-floored hall. Looking down the dimly lighted corridor, Lily saw that Dr. Jack was a muscular but short man, wearing blue coveralls and a pair of dirt-caked brown cowboy boots.

In the full light of the waiting room, however, Lily saw that Dr. Jack wasn't a man at all.

"Hey," she said. "I'm Dr. Jack Jennings. How you doing?" She extended her hand to shake. Her close-cropped brown hair and square jaw made it easy to mistake her for a man at a distance. But close up, the smoothness of her cheeks made it clear she was a woman. Lily shook her hand, which, while big, was too soft to be a man's.

"You okay?" Dr. Jack asked.

"Um . . . yeah. Fine." If Lily had seen a woman who looked like Jack at Piedmont Park in Atlanta, she barely would have noticed her. But here in Versailles, where most premenopausal women were hyperfeminine slaves to Mary Kay cosmetics and the tanning bed, seeing a butch was shocking — like seeing a bull-mastiff in a litter of poodles.

"You thought I was gonna be a man, didn't you?" Dr. Jack sized up Lily with clear blue eyes.

"Um . . . yeah, I guess so. Just from the name and all."

Dr. Jack looked stern suddenly. "Now I hope you don't think that being a woman makes me less of a vet."

"Oh, gosh, no," Lily said quickly. "I mean, I minored in women's studies in college." What an idiotic thing to say, she thought. But it was too late; she'd already said it.

"So . . . Mordecai's out in your car?"

"Uh-huh."

"Well, it looks like you've got your hands full with your little girl there." She looked down at Mimi. "Hi, doll face." She smiled at Mimi for a second, then looked back up at Lily. "So, if you'd give me your keys, I can just run out and get ole Mordecai for you."

Lily handed over the keys.

Jack flashed her a gap-toothed grin. "I'm not a car thief, I promise." She propped open the screen door and disappeared outside. In a couple of minutes, she was back, carrying the one-hundred-eighty-pound dog as if he weighed no more than Mimi. She nodded at Lily. "Why don't y'all just follow me back to the exam room?"

In the examination room, Dr. Jack set Mordecai down on a long metal table. "I'm not exactly Mordecai's favorite person, but he knows he's hurt and needs help, so he'll listen to reason." Mordecai emitted a low growl as Dr. Jack cleaned his injuries.

"How bad is it?" Lily asked.

"Could be worse. He's gonna need a few stitches, though. We'll numb him, sew him up, give him a tetanus shot. He'll be all right." She looked at Mimi, then at Lily. "The sewing part's not pretty, though. You can wait outside if you're squeamish."

Lily reached out to pat Mordecai's big head. "I'll stay, if it's okay. Just in case he wants me here."

"Sure." Dr. Jack opened the refrigerator in the corner, which was full of medicine bottles. She selected a bottle and closed the door. "So, if you don't mind me asking, how come you're the one bringing Mordecai in? Big Ben or Jeanie usually brings him."

Lily realized she hadn't introduced herself. "I kind of . . . inherited Mordecai. I married Big Ben and Jeanie's son, Benny Jack."

"Benny Jack McGilly finally got married?" She squinted at a syringe as she filled it with medicine. "Huh." She slipped the needle into a fold of Mordecai's flesh. He didn't even flinch.

"You're good at that," Lily said.

"I practiced that a lot in vet school . . . giving shots so they wouldn't hurt so much." She scratched one of Mordecai's ears. "Poor feller's already hurting, no need for me to make it worse. Actually, y'all are lucky I was in this afternoon. I got called out to the Weaver farm at four o' clock this mornin' to help a cow in calf. I was so beat at lunch today I thought about not coming back to the office this afternoon. I do large animal calls in the mornin', small animals in the afternoon." She gave Mordecai another affectionate scratch. "Not that you'd really call ole Mordy here a small animal."

Dr. Jack's grin was contagious, and Lily felt herself

smiling, too. "So do any of the local farmers act surprised when they see the vet's a woman?"

"Aah, I reckon they'd be surprised if it was any other woman, but my daddy was the county vet before me, and I used to go out with him on farm calls when I wasn't any bigger than a minute. Daddy raised me by himself, so he never wanted to leave me alone in the house when he took off in the middle of the night to help birth a colt or somethin'. So I always went with him. I was helping deliver farm babies when I was practically a baby myself. People just always figured I'd take over Daddy's practice when he retired." She lightly touched Mordecai's wounded foot. "He's numb. Time to sew him up. 'Scuse me if I don't talk during this part."

Dr. Jack's big hands worked deftly, neatly stitching together Mordecai's torn flesh. Mimi was getting restless, so Lily walked her around the exam room, pointing out the posters of puppies and kittens.

"Okay," Dr. Jack said, "one more shot, and ole Mordy'll be good to go." She looked down at Mimi as she went to retrieve more medicine from the refrigerator. "Is little doll face there Benny Jack's?"

"Uh-huh," Lily said, reminding herself to preserve the myth.

"Well, whaddaya know?" Dr. Jack cackled. "I wouldn'ta thought he had it in him." Her smile faded. "I didn't mean anything by that. I just meant —"

Lily smiled. "I think I know what you meant."

Their eyes locked for a moment, in the straightforward way that only gay people look at each other. I know what she is, Lily thought, but she's still trying to figure out what the hell I am . . . trying to reconcile the gaydar with the husband and baby.

Dr. Jack broke her gaze, rifled through a drawer, and produced a roll of bandages. "You'll need to change his bandage in the mornin'. Be sure to check that there's not any unusual discharge from the wound. If there is, call the office right away. He'll probably be in some pain today and tomorrow . . . you can slip in an aspirin in some hamburger meat, and that oughta help. If he seems to be doing okay, call me at the end of the week just to let me know how he's healing up. We can also set up an appointment to take out the stitches."

Their facades were back in place: professional and appropriately distant. "Thank you, doctor."

"I'll walk you out." Dr. Jack lifted Mordecai down from the table and gently held his collar as he hobbled, three-legged, down the hall.

"Okay," Dr. Jack said, as she sorted things out at the front desk, "Mordecai, you get a Milk-Bone. Mimi, you get a lollipop, and you, Mrs. McGilly" — she handed a computer printout to Lily — "get the bill."

Lily smiled. "Gee, thanks."

Dr. Jack returned her grin. "My pleasure, Mrs. McGilly."

As she wrote the check, Lily marveled at the direction her life was taking. She never thought she'd live to hear a butch — or anyone — call her "Mrs." anything.

After Lily finally agreed to let Mordecai in bed with her, he dropped off in a fitful sleep. Lying awake while Mordecai snored beside her and Ben snored in the next room, Lily had her first moment of enlightenment since Charlotte's death.

She was thinking about the story Dr. Jack told, about going with her father on vet calls when she was a little girl. There was a picture book in that story — a picture book about farm animals, so simple that even very young children like Mimi could enjoy it. But the pictures of the farm animals could be framed by the story of the little girl and her father — and how the little girl wants to grow up to be a vet.

Lily had never written a book for such young children before, but she liked the idea of writing something for Mimi. It would be a lasting gift for her daughter — even if things in the courtroom didn't work out.

She wanted to draw the animals in accurate detail, something along the lines of Garth Williams' wonderful illustrations for *Charlotte's Web*, but she hadn't been to a farm since a field trip in first grade. Lily wondered if Dr. Jack might agree to let her go along on a few farm calls, so she could sit back at a safe distance and sketch the animals. She would ask her on Friday, she decided, when she called about Mordecai.

Chapter 11

"The hearing is set for August fifteenth," Buzz Dobson told Lily and Ben as they sat in his dingy law office, the decor of which consisted of half a dozen dusty football trophies and one bedraggled plastic plant. "Let's just pray that the air-conditioning in the courthouse is working."

Lily sighed and looked down at Mimi, who was getting positively filthy playing on the law office's unmopped floor. "I'm afraid the temperature in the courtroom is the least of our worries."

Buzz shot Ben a conspiratorial grin. "She's the nervous type, ain't she?"

"Well," Ben said, attempting a macho attitude, "you know how women get about babies."

Lily sat quietly with her hands in her lap, but her fists were clenched so tightly she doubted anyone would be able to pry them apart.

Buzz pasted a condescending smile across his face. "Now, Mrs. McGilly, I don't think you have a thing to worry about. We just need to establish that you and Benny Jack love each other and that you love Mimi and take good care of her. And if Benny Jack here is Mimi's real father like he says he is, you've got no worries."

"Right," Lily said, clenching her fists even tighter. "No worries."

"Now if you wanna do something that'll turn the odds even more in your favor, I have a couple of suggestions for you, Mrs. McGilly."

"Yeah?"

"Well . . ." Buzz shuffled some papers uncomfortably. "When you're up there on the stand, you could try to look like a nice girl."

"A nice girl?" Lily looked down at her cutoff Levi's and Doc Martens, which were separated by pasty white legs whose unshaven state was due to apathy rather than feminist politics. "Well, I was planning on wearing a dress, if that's what you mean."

Buzz smiled self-consciously and reshuffled his papers. "Um, well, yes, that's part of it. But I was also thinking you could take that . . . that thing out of your nose and maybe do something with your hair."

"My hair?" Lily was proud of her hair. Very few white girls had such soulful braids.

111

"Yeah, I mean . . . somethin' respectable." He was still staring at his desk. "Look, Mrs. McGilly, I'm not a fashion expert, and the last thing I wanna do is tell a lady how she should fix herself up. I'm just saying that in these parts, a judge might look more sympathetically on a lady with a more . . . conservative appearance."

Lily flinched at the sound of the word *conservative* but muttered, "I'll see what I can do." As long as she was the same person on the inside, it didn't matter what clothes she wore or how she styled her hair. Or so she tried to convince herself. If the only way she could keep her daughter was by deceiving people with misleading appearances, then deceive them she would.

At first Lily had been reluctant when Ben had wanted to invite Ken over for dinner. The facade of propriety they had created was so delicate that the slightest provocation could cause it to shatter.

"Don't be so paranoid, O wife of mine," Ben had said. "Married couples have bachelor friends over for dinner all the time — just to make sure the poor single guys get a decent meal every once in a while. No one will think a thing of it. And besides," he added, "Ken knows the truth. Wouldn't it be nice to be able to let your guard down for an evening — to spend a few hours not pretending to be my little woman?"

Lily had to admit that it would.

Despite the fact that she was not slated to play the role of little woman for the evening, Lily still got saddled with the cooking. She didn't mind it, actually.

Ben's culinary abilities were limited to picking up the phone and ordering Chinese takeout, and there was no Chinese takeout to be had in Versailles.

So now, they — Lily, Ben, Ken, and Mimi — were sitting around the oak dining room table, eating Lily's vegetarian chili with cheese, sour cream, and flour tortillas. Mimi, in her high chair, was wearing a flour tortilla on her head.

Ken, who was quite attractive in a just-stepped-out-of-a-Ralph-Lauren-ad kind of way, took an appreciative bite of chili. "Quite a little cook you got here, Ben," he teased, winking at Lily. "You know what they say: The best way to a man's heart is his stomach."

Lily swigged the Corona and lime that Ken had brought to complement their meal. "Actually, I think the most direct route to a man's heart lies farther south."

Ben and Ken burst out laughing.

Finally, Ben said, "You sounded like Dez there for a second."

Lily smiled. "I did, didn't I?"

Ken turned to Ben. "Dez was your ex, right?"

"Yep." Ben pushed his empty bowl away. "We were lovers for eighteen months, then friends for a decade. Dez could be maddening, but he was funny as hell. Lily, do you remember when he went to that faculty Halloween party dressed as Mae West?"

"How could I forget it? I helped lace up his corset beforehand, which was no mean feat, let me tell you."

Ben laughed. "Three mai tais, and Dez was sprawled on top of the piano singing 'Frankie and Johnny,' to the utter mystification of the better part of Atlanta State's liberal arts faculty."

Ken laughed. "I take it that when he did this, he already had tenure?"

Lily smiled. "You take it correctly. Dez was always flamboyant, but never foolish." She looked over at Mimi, who had poked two eye-size holes in her flour tortilla and was wearing it as a mask. "And it was Dez's kind sperm donation that helped create little tortilla face over there."

Ken smiled at the little girl. "Hmm . . . this is quite a byzantine ruse you've constructed here. I bet the whole thing's exhausting."

"It is." Lily didn't realize how exhausted she was until Ken made that observation. It was only now, while she was relaxing in the company of a person with whom she and Ben could be honest, that she fully realized how strained and tiring their other social interactions were. It was only in the presence of other gay people that she and Ben could relax and be a family — the kind of family they really were.

"Yeah," Ben said, "in Atlanta I used to bitch all the time about the little dramas going on in the gay community . . . all the backbiting and gossip. Now that I'm away from all the gossip, though, it's like I'm dying for some. I find myself calling all the shallow queens I used to bitch about just so I can find out who's lusting after whom."

Ken laughed. "I do the same thing with my friends back in Nashville. I also find myself voraciously reading those glossy fag rags I used to make fun of when I lived in the city."

Lily drained her Corona. "Where do you get those magazines around here?"

Ken grinned sheepishly. "The mailman delivers them . . . in a plain brown wrapper, no less. I save all the back issues. If you like, I could bring over the ones I've read."

"You know, I'm scaring myself, but I think I'd really like that," Ben said, rising to clear the table.

"Me, too." Lily was helping Mimi out of her high chair. "I'm starved to death for news about my people . . . even if it's just idle chatter about who's shtupping who." A prickle of fear hit her. "Of course, we'd have to be careful not to leave those magazines lying around. God, I hate this! It makes me feel so self-loathing, even though I'm not."

They settled in the living room. Lily had to coax Mordecai off the couch with a Milk-Bone. Since his injury, he had made the couch his own personal sickbed. He would make room for Lily or Mimi to sit with him, but he growled ill-temperedly at Ben or anyone else who tried to join him there.

"You know," Ken said, sitting on the couch next to Ben and draping his arm around Ben's shoulders, "when Ben told me what you were doing, I really objected to it at first. It seemed to me that you were just catering to other people's prejudices." He watched Mimi stacking her wooden alphabet blocks. "But then I started thinking: If you fought the custody battle as an open lesbian, you'd lose your daughter. Mimi would lose her mother and be raised as some kind of psycho-Christian. Everybody would lose in that situation. And while I'm uncomfortable with this level of deception . . . well, some things are just too precious to lose, even if it is to make a political point."

Lily nodded in agreement. "Yeah, sometimes I think I'd be a better person if I'd made myself a martyr for the cause of gay rights, but the thing is, I wouldn't just be sacrificing myself. I'd be sacrificing

Mimi, too, and sentencing her to the same miserable, oppressive upbringing her mother had."

Without warning, the front door swung open, and a female voice drawled, "Knock-knock! Hello?"

Ben and Ken scooted apart just as Lily's vapid sisters-in-law, Sheila and Tracee, walked into the living room. Each was wearing a pricey-looking pastel warm-up suit and had her platinum curls pulled back in a perky ponytail.

"Hi," Lily said, finding it difficult to feign friendliness. One of the numerous downsides to this faux marriage was that the McGillys dropped by unexpectedly any time they felt like it.

"Ken," Ben said, doing an even worse job of masking his irritation than Lily was, "meet Sheila and Tracee, my sisters-in-law. Girls, I don't know if you remember Ken Woods. He went to high school with me."

Sheila nodded at Ken. "Your daddy used to work with State Farm Insurance, didn't he?"

"Sure did." Ken was doing an admirable job of being cordial.

"So . . . Sheila, Tracee, I was just about to make some coffee. Would you like some?" As grating as these drop-in visits were, Lily was determined not to alienate any of the McGillys through her lack of hospitality. After all, her success in the courtroom depended largely on the McGillys' continued good will.

"No thanks," Sheila chirped. "Me and Tracee just decided to have a night away from the boys — let them stay home with the kids for a change."

"There's this new aerobics class they're starting over at the middle school," Tracee added. "We thought we'd stop by to see if you wanted to come with us."

The idea of aerobics — let alone the idea of aerobics performed alongside Sheila and Tracee — filled Lily with the kind of anxiety she hadn't experienced since junior-high PE class. It wasn't that she was adverse to exercise. Back in Atlanta, she and Charlotte had taken long walks every evening, talking about the day's happenings and pushing Mimi in her stroller.

But walking was a natural exercise — it was something human beings were inclined to do anyway. There was nothing in Lily's genetic makeup, however, that gave her the inclination to contort her body in rhythm to outdated top-forty music. "Gosh, guys, I'd really love to, but as you can see, we have company."

"Oh, you go ahead." Ben smiled with devious benevolence. "Ken and I can hold down the fort here."

She looked at her ersatz husband with pure spite. She knew what that twinkle in his eyes was all about. He and Ken would be making out on the couch like a couple of teenagers, while she was forced to skip around a middle-school gym like a moron. "Well, I don't know, hon. Mimi still needs to be put to bed."

"Don't you worry about a thing." Ken smiled. "Daddy Ben and Uncle Ken will take care of her."

"Come on, Lil-leee," Sheila playfully whined, "it'll be *fun*."

Now she was in the position of looking like a total bitch if she declined. "Just a second . . . let me go get changed."

In her room, she threw on a baggy long-sleeve T-shirt and some cutoff sweatpants, all the while imagining elaborate ways to murder Ben and Ken. A mere five minutes ago, she had been having such a pleasant evening.

"I tell you what, Lily," Tracee said, after they had piled into her Lexus. "Five years ago, if Sheila and me was gonna have a girls' night out, we woulda been heading to the bars instead of to aerobics class."

Sheila giggled. "We're getting old, I guess."

"Yep," Tracee agreed, "we ain't nothin' but old married ladies. How 'bout you, Lily? You feel like an old married lady yet?"

"I don't know. I hadn't really given it much thought."

"Oh, you wait till Benny Jack knocks you up a couple times, then you'll feel like an old married lady — trust me." Tracee laughed.

Lily hoped her tight-lipped smile didn't reveal how uncomfortable she really was. She had spent very little time around straight women over the course of her adult life; it was little wonder she was so clueless about how to act like one.

The aerobics class was, if possible, even worse than Lily had imagined. The middle-school gym was populated by a herd of slim, tanned bleached-blond women who looked like so many Sheilas and Tracees. Lily wondered if somewhere in Faulkner County a factory churned out these seemingly identical women just as the Confederate Sock Mill churned out identical socks. The one distinctive-looking woman in the class was middle-aged and heavy, her broad hips stuffed into a pair of gray sweatpants.

Lily was just admiring the big woman's chutzpah for attending an aerobics class full of Sheilas and Tracees when the real Sheila elbowed her, nodded toward the big woman, and whispered, "Somebody's got a long way to go."

The aerobics instructor was distinctive from all the

Sheilas and Tracees only in that her hair was brunet. Her taut and toned body was apparent in her electric-blue leotard and hot-pink tights, and a zealous smile of the type worn by born-again Christians was plastered across her carefully made-up face. "O-*kay*, lay-deez!" she chirped, clapping her well-manicured hands. "We're gonna start in tonight with a weigh-in. And then, after you've been coming to this class for six weeks, we'll weigh in again, and you'll really see some improvement."

She led the way to the locker room, where the "ladies" were invited to come in one at a time to stand on the scales. Several of the Sheilas and Tracees giggled when the heavy woman took her turn, and one voice stage-whispered the word, "Tilt!" If there was a way in which this class was dissimilar to junior-high PE, Lily failed to see it.

As she stepped into the locker room for her turn on the scales, she even breathed in the odors of junior-high PE — the stale, sour smell of pubescent sweat. "O-*kay*, hon," the aerobics instructor, whom Lily had begun to think of as Spandex Dominatrix, said, "now, how tall are you?"

"About five-three."

Spandex Dominatrix wrote the information down on her clipboard. "Step on the scales, please."

Just as she would have when she was thirteen, Lily dumbly obeyed.

"Uh-huh," Spandex chided as she looked at the scale. "You're a full eight pounds over your ideal body weight. But don't worry. Stay in this class, and you'll be shedding that flab in no time!"

Lily walked out of the locker room, disgusted not because she was supposedly a few pounds over her ideal body weight, but because she had let Spandex Dominatrix actually make her feel bad about herself for a few seconds. Sheila and Tracee, she noticed, had stripped down to butt-floss leotards for their weigh-ins, and she saw the fat woman looking at their firm buttocks with a mixture of envy and loathing.

What was this psychosis American women had about weight? Even Lily, a supposedly enlightened feminist, fell prey to it sometimes. When she had suffered an insecure moment, when she had expressed to Charlotte the need to flatten her tummy or firm up her butt, Charlotte had always pulled her close and whispered, "Now, who wants to ride in a car that doesn't have any upholstery?"

The women lined up in rows for their exercises. "O-*kay*, lay-deez," Spandex Dominatrix chirped, like Richard Simmons with just a touch more estrogen, "we're gonna start out with a warmup. But first, does anybody have any questions before we start burning off those calories?"

Lily felt her hand go up in the air.

"Uh-huh?" Spandex acknowledged her.

"Uh . . . yeah." Lily searched for the right words. "I was just wondering, why does this class have to be about how skinny we can get? Can't we just exercise to improve our health and feel good instead of trying to live up to some impossible commercial ideal of beauty?"

Although Spandex was still wearing her smile, she was looking at Lily as though she had been speaking to her in Latvian. Finally, Sheila nodded toward Lily and said to the aerobics instructor, "She ain't from around here."

"Oh," Spandex Dominatrix said, seeming to find

Sheila's comment a satisfactory explanation. "O-*kay*, let's get started then."

The soundtrack for their stretching was, as Lily had suspected, moldy top forty. They moved from the warmup into a more strenuous step routine. Lily looked around to all the Sheilas and Tracees, who were clapping and yelling "Whoo-hoo!" and enjoying themselves enormously. Great, Lily thought . . . stepping with the Stepford Wives. She took some comfort in watching the fat woman, who at least looked appropriately miserable. It wasn't the exercise that was exhausting Lily; it was the fact that she was supposed to be perky while she was doing it.

In the car after the ordeal was over, Sheila said, "I can't believe what you said in class. I thought I was gonna die!"

"It's just cause you're a newlywed," Sheila said. "In a few years, you'll know how important it is to keep them pounds off . . . to keep Benny Jack's eye from wandering."

"Well," Lily said, feeling ridiculous even as she said it, "I like to think that Ben wants me for me, and not for my waist size."

Sheila and Tracee burst out laughing.

"Yeah," Tracee hooted, "you'd like to think that, wouldn't you?"

Lily entered the house to find Ben and Ken cuddling on the couch. "It's getting late," she barked. "Y'all can't be together at all hours of the night. People will talk."

"Damn," Ben said, "what's wrong with you? PMS or something?"

"Ben," Lily sighed, "how would you like it if you were forced to go out and play a game of tackle football with a bunch of straight boys who farted a lot and talked incessantly about pussy?"

"Uh . . . well, it sounds like my idea of hell," Ben said.

"Exactly. And I have just been to that same circle of hell for the opposite sex, with Sheila and Tracee as my guides." She nodded toward Ken. She really did like him, and didn't want to come off as a total psychopath. "I'm sorry I was rude, Ken. I enjoyed visiting with you tonight . . . before I got sucked into the vortex of doom. And now if you'll excuse me, I'm going to check on Mimi, take a shower, and have a nervous collapse."

Lily stood in the shower, the sound of the running water drowning out her sobs. There were only two things she wanted — Charlotte, and her old life back — and both of them were as impossible to retrieve as the water that went down the drain.

She knew one thing for sure. If she didn't find some lesbian friends soon, didn't find a safe place where she could hang out and be herself, she was going to lose her mind. She was not psychologically fit for this kind of intense, twenty-four-hour undercover work.

Chapter 12

"No oozing around the site of the injury?" Dr.
Jack's voice asked over the phone.

"No." Feeling her throat constrict around the
mouthful of yogurt she'd been trying to swallow, Lily
wondered if there was a more unpleasant word in the
English language than *oozing*.

"Any pus?" Dr. Jack asked, answering Lily's
unspoken question.

"No." Giving up on eating any yogurt herself, she
instead spooned it into Mimi's gaping mouth.

"Okay, then, why don't you just bring him into the

office in ten days, and we'll get those stitches out. If he has any problems before then, be sure and call me."

Lily knew that Dr. Jack was winding down their phone conversation, but she didn't want to let her go until she had asked her about another matter. "Dr. Jack?"

"Uh-huh."

"There was something else I wanted to talk to you about."

"Uh-huh?" She sounded puzzled.

"I, uh . . . I don't think I mentioned this to you the other day, but I write and illustrate — that is, draw the pictures —" She mentally kicked herself for explaining what *illustrate* meant. The *Dr.* in Dr. Jack's name meant she probably understood the meaning of three-syllable words. "Children's books."

"Is that a fact?" Dr. Jack sounded mildly interested, but still puzzled.

"Yeah. I was thinking about what you said about going on farm calls with your dad when you were a little girl, and I thought that a story about a little girl who did that might make a good picture book."

"Ha!" Dr. Jack laughed. "I don't think anybody's ever thought of me as literary material before." She was silent for a moment. "Seriously, though, I like the idea. Daddy died last year. A book like that might be a good way to remember him."

"We could even dedicate it to him if you wanted," Lily said.

"Hmm."

Lily waited for her to add something, but she never did. Finally she jumped in. "The thing is, I'm kind of a city girl, and I'd really need to spend some time around farm animals in order to draw them well. So I was wondering if maybe I could go on a few farm calls with you. I'd stay out of your way, of course —"

Dr. Jack laughed — a deep, low chuckle. "I don't know. A city girl has to get up pretty early in the mornin' to go on a farm call."

"I can handle that. I'm kind of a morning person anyway." That last part was a big lie, but she didn't want Dr. Jack to stereotype her as a night-owl urbanite.

"Well, you just keep your drawing things packed then, Mrs. McGilly, 'cause I'll be calling you one mornin' without any notice."

Lily hung up the phone and realized that the conversation had made her so nervous that she had been spooning yogurt into Mimi's mouth faster than she could eat it.

Dr. Jack hadn't been kidding about the early part. On Saturday morning, when the clock read four-seventeen, the phone rang. "Hello?" Lily croaked.

"Hey. I thought you said you were a mornin' person," Dr. Jack laughed. "Just got a call about a sow in trouble. You wanna come?"

"Sure, I guess so."

"You live on that road out by the Free Will Baptist, don'tcha?"

"Uh-huh."

"I'll come by and get you then. I'm on my way."

Lily threw on yesterday's clothes and splashed some water on her face. She bumped into Ben on her way out of the bathroom.

"Was it that bull dyke veterinarian on the phone?" he asked, rubbing his heavy-lidded eyes.

"Now, now, dear, that's not a very politically correct way to refer to her."

"Nobody who calls at four o'clock on a Saturday morning gets the PC treatment," Ben muttered.

"I shouldn't be gone long," Lily said. "I don't think Mimi will wake up before I get back, but if she does, you can look after her, right?"

"Hey, what are self-proclaimed fathers for?"

Dr. Jack came to fetch Lily in a faded red Chevy pickup. It was impossible to imagine her driving anything else. "Hop on in, Mrs. McGilly," she said, grinning. Dr. Jack, clearly a morning person, looked alert and cheerful despite the fact that it wasn't even five a.m.

"Please call me Lily." Pretty please, she thought.

"Lily McGilly!" Dr. Jack laughed.

"Trust me. You're not the first person to find my married name amusing."

"I guess not. Well, some folks call me Jack, and some folks call me Doc. You take your pick — just as long as you don't call me by my given name."

"Which is?"

"Jacqueline. My momma got it outta some book she was reading. It never did suit me. Her giving me that name was just like her putting me in frilly dresses all the time. Pretty things just don't suit me. I was always the plain, practical type. Not like Momma."

"Is your mother still alive?"

"As far as I know. 'Course, the last time I heard anything was probably four years ago. She was still living down in Florida then. That's where she went when she left Daddy and me. She left Daddy for another man when I was seven years old, but she didn't stay with him either. She couldn't be satisfied with nothin' . . . she was the restless type. I think that's one of the things that got on her nerves about Daddy and me: We were both content to stay in the same place and do the same thing. Not a restless bone in our bodies."

"Hmm," Lily said. "I think a lot of women in your mother's generation were probably dissatisfied, always thinking they'd be happier with some other man, when the source of their unhappiness was really a lot deeper than that."

"Huh," Jack said. "You think a lot."

Lily blushed. She hadn't meant to get all theoretical, but she had just the same. All those years of living with a college professor, maybe. "I guess I do. Maybe it's because I'm a writer. Of course, I don't tend to philosophize like that in my books, since my usual audience is made up of seven-year-olds."

Jack grinned. "You know, when you asked me if you could come along on some farm calls, I kinda wondered if you'd be a nuisance, since I'm so used to being by myself. But having some company for a change is nice."

"We've not even gotten to the farm yet. I've still got plenty of time to be a nuisance." It occurred to her that she had absolutely no idea what to expect when they arrived. "Say, when you called you said there was a sow in trouble. What did you mean by that? It sounded like she'd been caught writing bad checks or something."

Jack laughed. "No, a pig's too smart to get caught writing bad checks. This sow's in labor, but she can't

get one of the piglets pushed out. It happens sometimes — a baby'll get turned the wrong way in the
birth canal. And the mother panics cause she doesn't
know what's going on. It's really just a matter of
getting the piglet turned around the right way. It's not
hard if you know what you're doing."

Jack pulled the truck into a long gravel driveway
at the end of which was a small, white frame house.
The house was dwarfed by the huge, unpainted barn
that sat behind it.

A craggy-faced man in a John Deere cap and
overalls began talking to Jack before she could even
get out of the truck. "She's in the barn over yonder. I
done got you some soap and hot water."

"Thanks, Ed. Let's go take a look at her."

Jack was apparently in an all-business mood, since
she didn't bother introducing Lily to the farmer.
Figuring that manners took the backseat in a medical
crisis, Lily grabbed her sketch pad and pencils and
tagged along behind Jack and Ed, feeling faintly
ridiculous.

The sweet hay smell of the barn was soured by
sounds of fear and pain. In a corner pen, the
enormous sow paced and squealed. Her eyes were wild,
terrified. Two newborn piglets lay a few feet away
from her, tiny and pink, rooting blindly in the straw.

This was the first birth Lily had attended since
Mimi's, and while the mother pig didn't have as
colorful a vocabulary as Charlotte, the similarities
between the two occasions were striking. Lily knew
the party line was that giving birth was a beautiful
thing, and she agreed with that sentiment up to a
point. But the miracle of birth also had a dark, scary
side. One only needed to look at the panicking sow

and her frail piglets to remember that all living creatures are born helpless, out of their mother's fear and pain.

Lily kept her distance and watched the vet do her work.

Jack began by scrubbing her hands in the basin of hot water Ed had provided. She nodded toward the sow. "Now, Ed, this un's named Minnie, right?"

He nodded.

"I like how you name all your livestock, Ed," she said, climbing into the pen. "It makes it easier when I've got somethin' to call 'em." She leaned down so the pig could see her. "Now, Minnie. You take it easy, ole girl. You're gonna be just fine." She looked up at Ed. "Hey, Ed, you got any little treats you could hand-feed this girl? Food's better than anesthesia to a pig."

Ed disappeared and returned shortly with a bowl of sliced apples.

"That oughta do the trick," Jack said. "Ed, you hold her steady for me. Lily, why don't you come over here and feed Minnie some apple? If you're gonna draw her, you might as well get acquainted with her."

Lily approached the pen reluctantly. "Uh, what if she bites me?"

Jack laughed. "I can't believe you've got that big monster of a dog at your house, and you're scared of a pig biting you. Just put the apple in your palm and hold your hand flat. That way she won't be able to get ahold of your hide."

My *hide*? Lily thought, but she did as she was told. Minnie slurped the apple slice off her hand gratefully.

While Lily concentrated on the sow's mouth, Jack

squatted down at its opposite end and rolled up the sleeves of her coveralls. "Keep those apple slices coming, Lily. I'm about to do somethin' the ole girl's not gonna appreciate a bit."

Lily dutifully served up the apple, glad that she was dealing with the preferable end of the pig.

"No wonder that piglet's stuck, Ed. It's trying to back out of her."

"It still alive?" Ed asked.

"Yup," Jack muttered. "Won't be for long, though, if we don't get it out."

Lily doled out more apple while Jack rummaged around in the pig's nether regions. "Damn," Jack said. "She's tight in there. Being scared's caused her to seize up, I reckon." Jack moved around in an attempt to get a better angle. "Damn it, Ed, would you believe my hand's too big to get a grip on the little fella?" She groped around a few more seconds, then said, "Hey, Lily, would you come here a minute?"

"What for?"

"I want you to wash your hands, then see if you can get a grip on this piglet."

Lily shuddered. Knowledge of animals' insides was definitely not required in order to draw them for a picture book. "I was having a hard enough time just feeding her this apple."

"It's either you try to do it or I kill this piglet so the others can get out."

Lily rose and scrubbed her hands. She was squeamish as hell about getting so intimate with a hoofed creature, but as a vegetarian, she was supposedly devoted to protecting animal life.

Jack gestured toward the pig's orifice. "Now if you

can just wedge your hand in so you can get a good grip around the piglet's middle, you can pull it right out."

"Sorry, Minnie," Lily mumbled as she shoved her hand into the sow's vagina. "Usually I at least buy a girl dinner before we get to this part."

As Lily groped around in the darkness, she suddenly felt the warmth and movement of a living creature. The piglet was wedged in tight, but she slowly worked her hand alongside it, and then painstakingly turned her wrist until she was gripping the animal just behind what felt like its back legs. "Got it . . . I think."

"Okay," Jack said. "Now pull, but go easy."

Gripping the tiny animal firmly, Lily brought her arm back in a slow, steady pull. The piglet's curly tail was visible first, then finally its wet pink ears and snout. "It's breathing!" Lily cried, overcome with the emotion of the moment. "Is it a boy or a girl?"

Jack glanced under the pig's tail. "Looks like a girl."

Ed looked at Lily and laughed. He apparently wasn't used to seeing someone get so worked up over livestock.

"Well, it sure is," Jack said. "Ed, I reckon you'll have to name this piglet Lily . . . after her midwife."

Ed grinned. "You're plum crazy, Doc . . . not changed a lick since you was a little girl."

Jack grinned back. "Why don't you get us some more hot water so we can wash up? I'll stay till all the piglets are born, but my guess is the rest of the delivery will go normally."

It did go normally. Minnie lay on her side and

squeezed out piglet after piglet, until the litter totaled seven. Lily sketched the pigs while Jack kept the apple slices coming.

"How they doing?" Ed asked when he returned with fresh water.

"They look great," Jack said.

"Well, Vina's got some breakfast cooked, if y'all wanna eat before you go."

"You know me," Jack said, scrubbing her hands. "I wouldn't miss one of Vina's breakfasts. They're this job's number-one fringe benefit."

Lily sat with Jack at the table in Ed and Vina's spotless kitchen, with the morning sun shining through the red-and-white gingham curtains. The table was spread with an artery-clogging breakfast buffet: hot biscuits, red-eye gravy, cooked apples, fried eggs, grits, ham, bacon, and sausage.

"Now you girls eat all the biscuits you want," Vina, a smiling, plump woman said, filling their mugs with coffee. "I just put another pan in the oven."

"Thanks, but I'm sure one pan will be plenty," Lily said. But after she saw the way Jack was filling up her plate, she wasn't so sure anymore. She bit into a biscuit and surveyed the numerous pig products on the table uneasily. "So," she said, "what's gonna happen to my piggy namesake after she grows up?"

"Same thing that happens to most pigs, I reckon," Ed said, spearing a sausage patty.

"Oh." The thought of the little piglet surviving a difficult birth only to wind up on someone's breakfast table depressed Lily. The piglet's plight seemed similar to Mimi's. Lily mourned for small creatures who had no control over their destinies. She was embarrassed to feel a tear sliding down her cheek.

"You city girls get softhearted about animals, don'tcha?" Ed asked, pouring gravy over a split biscuit.

"Sorry," Lily said, feeling foolish. "It just struck me as sad, is all."

"Well, shoot," Jack said, helping herself to a third fried egg. "If you're gonna get that upset about it, I reckon Ed and Vina can just bring Lily the pig out to me after she gets weaned. I'll pay as good a price for her as they will at the meat market, and I reckon I've got room on my farm for a pig."

"You and your farm," Vina laughed, emptying the second pan of biscuits into the bread basket.

"Ed and Vina always make fun of my farm," Jack began. "Of course, I reckon they've got a right to. It's more of a petting zoo than a farm. I've got half a dozen dogs — some I found on the side of the road, some I took away from people that was mistreating 'em; five cats; an old swaybacked horse I saved from getting shot; and a goat with just one horn. You oughta bring your little girl out to see 'em."

Lily smiled. "I'll have to do that."

"Anyway," Jack said as she spooned up another serving of grits, "I reckon I got room for a pig in my collection, if you and Mimi promise to come visit her."

"I promise."

"It sure takes a lot of money to feed all them animals without you making any profit off 'em," Ed said, pushing his plate away.

"Aah, it's not that expensive," Jack said. "Besides, I gotta spend my money on somethin'. It's not like I go out and blow it on new dresses."

Ed and Vina laughed. Lily was amazed at how comfortable they were with Jack's masculinity.

When they climbed into the truck to go home, Lily said, "Thank you for the pig."

"It was no skin off my nose. I'd been thinking about getting me a pig anyhow." She started the truck. "And I can understand why the thought of slaughtering that pig bothered you. I mean, I'm no vegetarian, but it does seem like a shame that a critter has such a hard time coming into the world, only to get taken out of it so quick." She watched the road for a minute. "There was somethin' I wanted to ask you, though."

"Yeah?"

"About that joke you made when you were about to invade that sow's privacy."

"Oh, that. I hardly even knew what I was saying. I always make dumb jokes when I'm nervous."

"Well, it's probably none of my business. It just seemed like an odd joke for a married lady to be making . . . at least for a married lady who's married to a man."

The biscuits in Lily's stomach congealed into a heavy clump. How could she be so stupid as to make a joke like that? Apparently waking up before the sun wasn't conducive to her secret-keeping abilities.

"It's okay," Jack said. "Like I said, it's none of my business. You don't have to tell me anything. But if you ever decide you wanna talk, your secrets — if you've got any — are safe with me."

What was it about Dr. Jack that made Lily decide to trust her? Was it because she was the first real lesbian Lily had seen since she hit Faulkner County? Or was it Jack's obvious kindness — the part of her personality that made her rescue abused dogs and swaybacked horses?

134

Whatever it was, it made Lily talk. She talked all the way back to the house and then sat talking with Jack in her truck in the driveway.

When Lily finished, Jack breathed, "Whoa. That's quite a story."

Lily laughed. "You're telling me."

"So . . ." Jack looked her square in the eye. "You lonely?"

Lily quickly broke eye contact. "Lonely? Of course I'm lonely. I lost my wife, my best friend — but if you're, like, coming on to me, I'm not interested. The only thing that could possibly make my life more complicated than it is now is a relationship. Besides, I'll never find anyone I can love like I loved Charlotte —"

"Whoa, Nelly!" Jack hollered. "Let me try again. What I meant to say was you probably had lots of friends back in Atlanta . . . other dykes you hung out with. I bet that now that you're away from them, you're kinda lonely."

"Oh. That kind of lonely." Lily felt like an idiot. Why had she gotten so defensive? "Yeah, I guess I am lonely. Sometimes, it's nice, you know, just to hang out with other dykes and talk about dyke things."

"Yeah, I know what you mean. My friend Honey runs a tattoo shop out on Peacock Alley. She's got an apartment out back, and Friday nights a bunch of us go out there . . . just to hang out and be dykes, like you said. There's Honey and her girlfriend and a couple of old army dykes from Fort Oglethorpe. They're all older than you are — on the wrong side of forty, like me — but we'd be glad to have you if you think your husband wouldn't mind you having a girls' night out."

"I bet he wouldn't. God knows he's been having

boys' nights out often enough. So where is this Peacock Alley?"

"That's not really the name of the road. That's just what locals call the old highway that runs between here and Chattanooga. It's called Peacock Alley because years ago, when it was a main road, there used to be all these roadside stands that sold those chenille bedspreads with gaudy-colored peacocks on 'em. Those bedspreads'd be hanging on clotheslines, blowing in the breeze. I guess they were tacky, but when I was a little kid, I thought they were beautiful."

Lily pictured Jack as a young tomboy, watching the chenille peacocks fluttering in the breeze.

"You look like you wanna ask me somethin'," Jack said. "Go ahead. I've already made you tell me your life story."

"I was just wondering . . . people around here, like Ed and Vina . . . do they know about you?"

Jack grinned. "I guess so. I'm not the type to say much about my personal life, but I've never bothered to keep it much of a secret either. I think folks in Faulkner County think I'm the way I am on accounta my momma leaving and my daddy not knowing how to raise a girl. So I think they feel sorry for me." She rolled her eyes. "Not that there's anything to feel sorry for. Of course, given the choice, I guess I'd rather have them pity me than beat me up."

"Have you ever thought of moving away?"

"I did move away for a while — went to college in Chattanooga, then vet school in Knoxville. But I love my farm, and I always knew I'd wind up taking over

Daddy's practice. Besides, it doesn't matter if I live in a small town or a big town. Dykes turn any town into a small town."

Lily laughed. "I think you've got something there." She looked at her Timex. She had been gone a little over three hours. "Well, I'd better go inside. I want to be there when Mimi wakes up."

"Okay, well, nice talking to ya. I'll call you the next time I go to work on somethin' other than pigs. I figure you've drawn your fill of pigs. And hey, maybe I'll see you over at Honey's next week?"

"Maybe so. Bye."

Lily entered the living room to see Ben sitting on the sofa, bleary-eyed, still dressed in his T-shirt and boxers. Mimi was wide awake, playing a game that seemed to involve somersaulting over the reclining Mordecai while giggling a lot.

"She . . . woke . . . up . . . fifteen minutes . . . after you left," Ben droned. His usually perfectly coiffed hair was as unruly as Mimi's. "The first thing she said was, 'Mama gone, B-Jack. Let's play.' And that's what we've done, nonstop, for the past three and a half hours. God, taking care of a baby is, like, really tiring, isn't it?"

"There's a news flash." Lily ran a hand through his spiky hair. "You go back to bed if you want. I've got her."

He trudged back to his bedroom, as if shell-shocked from the unaccustomed childcare.

"Mama!" Mimi stretched out her arms and hurried toward Lily at a tippy-toeing toddler run.

Lily scooped up her daughter and held her on her

lap. "Guess what I did this morning, Mimi-saurus. I stuck my hand straight up a pig's patootie!"

"Piggy tootie!" Mimi repeated, and collapsed in a fit of giggles.

Chapter 13

Lily had been a good girl all week. On Sunday, she had made the potato salad for yet another of the McGillys' infernal family barbecues. On Tuesday, she had taken Granny McGilly to the optometrist in Callahan, even though she had gone on a five A.M. farm call with Jack that morning and so had gotten only five hours' sleep. On Wednesday, she had even gone to aerobics with Sheila and Tracee again. All week, she had been nothing but a dutiful imitation wife, granddaughter-in-law, and sister-in-law. And she, for one, was sick of it.

Ben, Lily knew, was equally tired of playing the respectable small-town family man. This week, when he could have been spending time with Ken, he had been pressured to lunch with Big Ben and his Rotary Club pals, and he halfheartedly had joined in their witticisms about the demands of married life.

It was out of Lily and Ben's exhaustion with "the demands of married life" that Lily's idea for a "romantic overnight getaway" was born. Last night, while picking at pasta and complaining about the agonies of compulsory heterosexuality, Lily had thought aloud, "Hmm . . . I wonder if your mom would be willing to keep Mimi overnight."

"I'd venture to say that nothing would make her happier than having an extended length of time in which to dress her granddaughter in frills and stuff her full of junk food. Why do you ask?"

"I don't know . . . I was just thinking, I'm sure you'd like to spend some time with Ken, and there's this get-together thing tomorrow night that Jack told me about . . . all dykes, apparently."

"So what are we going to tell my mom? That I'm hoping to finally have sex with this guy I've been dating, while you go and familiarize yourself with the Faulkner County, Georgia, chapter of the lesbian nation?"

"Actually, I was thinking we could put it in the terms of a romantic overnight trip. After all, we've been under so much stress lately with the hearing coming up . . . maybe we want to go away for a night, have some time just for the two of us."

"Boy, it's true what they say about women being devious, isn't it?" Ben laughed. "Let's do it."

A pinprick of worry stung Lily's brain. "Of course, it would be the first time I've left Mimi overnight."

"Hey, don't worry about that. Mom raised three unruly boys to adulthood; she's perfectly capable of taking care of one tiny girl."

Lily couldn't push back her anxiety. "But what if something goes wrong and we're not where we've said we are?"

"I'll tell you what. Ken has a friend who runs a bed-and-breakfast just north of Atlanta. Ken's been dying to take me there. If he can get us a room for tomorrow night, we could give Mom the bed-and-breakfast's number. If she calls me there, I'll call you where you are, and you can go see to Mimi."

"Okay, but you have to remember: If the phone rings in your room, you answer it, not Ken." Lily felt as if she had to resort to the tactics of a double agent just to have a normal evening out. "God, our lives are complicated."

"Yup." Ben flashed one of his uncharacteristically wide smiles. "But I'll tell you what. I'm willing to resort to all manner of subterfuge to make tomorrow night possible. I've been dreaming about a night alone with Ken Woods since I was a freshman in high school!"

The old road known by the locals as Peacock Alley was a ghost road, marked by crumbling monuments to the tourist trade of the days before the construction of the interstate. Low-slung motor courts with signs announcing AIR CONDITIONING, COLOR TV, and

VACANCY dotted the road, and Lily marveled that these little places managed to stay in business. She imagined that the family vacation motels of yesterday became the sites of today's clandestine trysts.

A clapboard building with a Confederate flag-bearing sign proclaiming JOHNNY REB'S SOUVENIRS made Lily think of the chenille peacock bedspreads that gave this road its nickname. The windows had been painted with yellow block letters reading BEDSPREADS, DISHWARE, and CIVIL WAR GIFTS. Lily couldn't tell if the store was closed for the day or for good.

As she drove north, toward Fort Oglethorpe, the roadside attractions took on a seedier appeal. Concrete block taverns called SHOOTERS and COWBOY'S appeared to be doing a good business, judging from the number of pickup trucks in the parking lot. One bar, the PINK PUSSYCAT, even claimed to have EXOTIC DANCERS. Lily wondered what passed for *exotic* in rural northern Georgia.

On her right, exactly where Jack said it would be, was a small brick building with a large sign announcing TATTOOS BY HONEY. Smaller signs on the store's windows proclaimed, HEALTH BOARD APPROVED and TATTOOS WHILE U WAIT. Lily pulled into the small gravel parking lot and took a deep breath.

Walking into a roomful of people had never been her favorite thing, and since Jack's red truck was nowhere to be seen, she'd be walking into a room full of strangers. She considered going home for a dull evening alone with Mordecai, but finally said to herself, "Goddamn it, if I can do aerobics with a bunch of straight Southern Baptist women, surely I can find the courage to walk into a roomful of dykes."

She walked around to the rear of the building, as Jack had told her to do, and knocked on the back door. It felt so secretive. She wondered if there was a secret password, like *Sappho* or something.

A full-figured, fortyish woman with wavy, naturally golden hair answered the door. Lily noticed right away that the woman's arms were completely covered by tattoos: a medieval unicorn resting in a garden of vibrantly colored flowers, a fairy with diaphanous wings sprinkling stardust with her magic wand, and a frog in a golden crown squatting philosophically on a lily pad. The designs were more fanciful than what Lily would have chosen for herself, but the artwork was undeniably beautiful.

"Hey," the woman said, grinning. Her face was as round, flat, and wide-eyed as a Persian cat's. "You must be Lily."

"Um . . . yeah. I didn't know you'd be expecting me."

"Jack said you might come by. I kinda recognized you 'cause I didn't recognize you. We don't see many new faces round here." She opened the door wider. "Come on in and meet the gang. I'm Honey, by the way."

"Nice to meet you. Love your sleeves."

Honey surveyed her tattooed arms with genuine pride. "Thanks. Designed 'em myself. Here, let me introduce you to the usual suspects here. The ingrate hogging the La-Z-Boy over there's Mick. She's my old man."

"Hey." Mick raised her Bud tallboy in a half toast. Her hair was cut in a salt-and-pepper dyke spike, and she wore a black Harley-Davidson T-shirt and a black leather jacket — a shocking fashion choice, given that

Honey's apartment was cooled only by two oscillating fans, which were doing nothing more than stirring the hot, soupy air.

"And over here's Dale and Sue."

On the overstuffed tan sofa sat a couple who were at least as old as Granny McGilly. The butch member of the duo — Dale, Lily presumed — had close-cropped, snow-white hair and wore a Georgia Bulldogs jersey and sweatpants. The femme's silver hair was shampooed and set, and she wore a lilac shell top with matching slacks. She put a long cigarette to her lips, and Dale dutifully leaned over to light it.

"Hey, babe," Sue said to Lily, her voice a husky smoker's rasp.

"Lord, girl, how old are you?" Dale asked, her voice having all the subtlety and modulation of Big Ben McGilly's. "Seventeen?"

Lily smiled. "Twenty-nine, actually."

"What a coincidence!" Dale whooped. "Me, too!"

"Don't you pay no attention to her," Sue said to Lily. "I ain't heard a word she's said in thirty years. I just keep her around 'cause she lights my cigarettes."

"Now, I'm good for a little more than that," Dale teased, letting her hand rest on Sue's knee.

"Oh, that's right." Sue waved her cigarette for emphasis. "You do take the trash out. I forgot about that."

Lily laughed. Butch/femme, it seemed, had never gone out of style in northern Georgia. Lily had always enjoyed the butch/femme dynamic in a postmodern, theatrical, and mainly reserved-for-the bedroom kind of way. But these women played their roles without a trace of irony.

Settling down in a nest of oversize floral-print

cushions on the floor, Lily wondered what the hyper-politically correct women at Athena's Owl Bookstore in Atlanta would make of these dykes. Would they think these rural women were living their lives according to oppressive patriarchal standards?

Who cares if they are? Lily thought. The two couples obviously loved each other, and the sexual sparks between them were warming up the room faster than the Georgia summer heat. Lily ached for Charlotte.

Honey was sitting on the arm of the La-Z-Boy, running her sky-blue nail-polished fingers through Mick's hair. "You wanna beer, Lily?" she asked, when she caught Lily looking at her.

"Yeah, a beer would be great, thanks."

Honey sashayed over to the fridge, which, along with a sink and stove, was in the far end of the living room. It was a tiny apartment. Lily could give herself the grand tour while sitting in one place and pivoting her head. A closed door next to the couch led to what she assumed was the bathroom. A door with a beaded curtain led to the bedroom, where Lily could see a queen-size bed covered with one of the chenille pea-cock bedspreads Jack had described. It really was gorgeous, in a garish sort of way.

The walls of Honey's apartment were hung with posters depicting dragons, unicorns, fairies, and wizards, and the small bookcase beside Lily housed a collection of science fiction and fantasy paperbacks.

When Honey brought Lily her beer, Lily asked, "You like Marion Zimmer Bradley?"

"Oh, lord," Mick groaned, lighting up a Marlboro Red. "Don't get her started talking about that crap."

"Mick's not much of a reader," Honey explained.

"She don't care about nothin' but riding around with that big ole Harley-Davidson vibrator between her legs."

Suddenly there was a pounding at the screen door and a gruff voice yelling, "I heard there was a buncha dykes holed up in here!"

Lily stiffened at the perceived threat.

Honey rolled her eyes and laughed. "That's just Jack. For somebody with a *Doctor* in front of her name, she acts like she don't have a brain in her head." She turned toward the door and hollered, "Get on in here, you crazy woman!"

Jack swung the door open wide. She was wearing faded Levi's and a crisp white, button-down shirt. It was the first time Lily had seen her wearing something other than coveralls and mud-caked boots.

"Hey, y'all." Jack yanked a can of Bud from the six-pack she was carrying and put the rest of the cans in the fridge. "Lily," she said, grinning broadly. "Glad you could make it."

"Glad to be here." Lily watched as Jack made a quick circuit of the room, shaking hands with Mick and Dale, giving Honey and Sue courtly kisses on the hand. To Lily's surprise, Jack settled down on the floor next to her, making the room a study in butch/femme pairings.

Lily knew that Jack sitting next to her shouldn't make her nervous — after all, Jack was the only person in the room whom she'd met before tonight — but it still did, and she found herself knocking back her beer a lot quicker than was probably good for her.

"Hey, Jack," Honey said, "you'll never guess who I ran into over at the Piggly Wiggly the other day."

"Oh, I bet I can guess," Jack laughed. "Was it Sandy?"

"Sure was. She's as pregnant as a cow, too."

Jack shook her head. "I'm not surprised. Sandy never does anything halfway. When she decided she was straight, I knew she was gonna be squeezing out pups as soon as nature would allow it."

"Sandy used to be a regular at these little get-togethers," Mick explained to Lily. "Her and Jack was together for a while, but then ole Sandy kinda retreated to the enemy camps."

"She went back to her ex-husband," Jack added. "Decided that what she was doing with me was just an 'experiment' . . . like I was her chemistry project or somethin'."

Honey laughed. "I wonder what she did about that pink triangle I tattooed on her ass. I notice she ain't had the guts to come back here and ask me to cover it up."

"Oh, I'm sure that dumb redneck husband of hers ain't even noticed it," Sue drawled. "And if he has, she probably told him it's just a birthmark he hadn't noticed before. I'm sure he'd be stupid enough to believe it."

Dale laughed and draped her arm around Sue's shoulders. "Lily, I bet you think we're awful. You're sitting there thinking, 'These country dykes don't do nothin' but sit around and drink beer and talk bad about people.'"

"Hey, drinking beer and talking bad about people are two of my favorite things." To illustrate her point, Lily popped open her second tallboy.

"Well, you'll fit right in here, then," Sue said.

"Actually, Lily, being from the city, you probably don't think we've got any educational stuff around here," Dale said. "But right while you're sitting here, you're looking at a natural history exhibit."

Lily knew she was being teased, but played along. "And what's that?"

Dale grinned. "Why, you're looking right at the oldest known lesbian couple in the history of Faulkner County, Georgia."

"That's great," Lily said, her insides aching as she thought of all the times she'd imagined growing old with Charlotte. "How long have you two been together?"

Sue squeezed Dale's age-spotted hand. "We met at the WAC training base in Fort Oglethorpe in nineteen and forty-four. I had a boyfriend back home, but when I first saw Dale, I knew I was through with the boys."

Dale smiled slyly. "Our first weekend pass, we checked into a hotel in Chattanooga and didn't come outta that room for two whole days."

Sue slapped Dale's leg. "Now don't go telling that!"

"A while back," Dale said, "when all that gays-in-the-military foolishness was going on, I couldn't help laughing. The military's brought more dykes together than any of them silly women's music festivals has."

"Hey, I went to one of them once," Honey protested. "It was fun."

Dale shook her head. "Not my kinda music."

"Not mine neither," Mick added. "When Honey dragged me to that thing, I thought I was gonna die of heat stroke or boredom, one. All that guitar strumming and singing about sisterhood . . . I had to play nothin' but Allman Brothers records for a week just to get all that strumming outta my head."

"You liked Glenda Mooney, though," Honey said, playing with the collar of Mick's leather jacket.

"She was all right. At least she played somethin' that had a beat to it."

"Say, Honey," Sue said, "speaking of music, why don't you put on that record Dale and me like?"

"Oh, lord, not that thing," Mick grumbled.

"Don't be rude, baby." Honey rose, sorted through a stack of LPs, and pulled out one marked "Love Song Canteen."

"I'll Be Seeing You" began to play, and Dale and Sue rose and began to dance. They held each other close and moved together in a light two-step. Dale led.

"Come on, Mi-ick." Honey was trying to drag her girlfriend out of the recliner.

"This ain't the kinda music I can dance to."

Honey rolled her eyes in exasperation. "Damn it, Mick, there ain't no *can* or *can't* to it. It's just hugging set to music."

Mick knocked back the rest of her beer and reluctantly stood up. Soon, though, she was resting her hands on Honey's ample hips, and Honey's hands had disappeared beneath Mick's black leather jacket.

On one level, it was comforting to be in a place where women could dance together — a safe place (albeit a hot and tiny place) where dykes could be dykes together. On a deeper level, though, watching those women dance just made Lily more aware of her own loneliness. Looking at Mick and Honey, she wondered what her life would have been like in ten years, had Charlotte lived. And looking at Dale and Sue only reminded her that she would never have the pleasure of growing old with the only woman she had ever loved.

The song "I'll Be Seeing You," a wartime ballad about how love lives on even after the loved one's death, wasn't exactly helping Lily's emotional state. She wiped what she thought was sweat running down her face only to discover it was a tear.

She jumped when Jack nudged her.

"Say," Jack whispered, "you wanna dance?"

Lily was grateful that Jack didn't ask her if she was okay, which was an obvious question with an even more obvious answer. "Uh . . . I don't know."

"I promise I'll be a perfect gentleman, what with you being a married lady and all."

Lily felt herself smile. "Oh, okay. What the hell?"

Lily stood up with Jack, who rested her hands on the small of Lily's back. Lily draped her arms over Jack's shoulders, and they began to gently sway.

"I haven't danced like this since high school," Lily said.

"Did you dance like this with boys?"

"Yup — pimply-faced little Beta Club boys." Lily laughed self-deprecatingly. "I didn't have a clue about myself back then. Once I got to college, though, I caught on pretty quick."

Jack laughed. "I was different than you, I guess. I always knew what I was, but I had the good sense not to do anything about it till I was in college."

"That was probably wise. I doubt that Faulkner County would be too tolerant of a sexually active teenaged lesbian."

"Lord, no, particularly since that was, what? Twenty-four years ago?" She grinned. "Of course, I might have showed good sense waiting till I was in college, but as soon as I started dating, my good sense went straight out the window. I went out with

anything with a pair of tits and a homosexual urge —
all the way through college in Chattanooga, then
through vet school in Knoxville. Sometimes I think the
entire population of Tennessee consists of my ex-
girlfriends."

Lily laughed. "I guess you had to slow down after
you moved back here."

"Oh, yeah, that was probably the best thing for
me, though. It made me grow up — have real relation-
ships instead of flings. Honey and I were together for
a while years ago, before Mick rode into town on her
Harley."

"Oh, yeah?" One of Lily's favorite things about
lesbians was their ability to turn ex-lovers into
platonic family members — and to welcome the ex-
lover's new partner into the family as well.

"And then, of course, there was Sandy."

Lily smiled. "You were her experiment, I believe?"

"Yup, that's me. And then she cast me aside like a
frog she was finished dissecting."

When the record of '40s music ended, Mick
hollered, "Thank god that's over! Honey, why don't
you put on some Allman Brothers — I've gotta get the
taste of that sweet stuff outta my mouth."

When the evening began to turn toward heavy
beer drinking and rock 'n' roll, Dale and Sue rose to
leave. "Well, we'd better take off," Sue said. "We old
ladies like to get to bed early."

Dale grinned. "Of course, that don't mean we
always get to sleep right away." She ducked as Sue
playfully slapped at her with her purse.

After they left, Lily said, "God, I guess it sounds
condescending to call them adorable, but they really
are."

"Oh yeah, they're great," Honey agreed. "I always call them my lesbian grandmas." Honey grabbed more beers for the four of them. "So," she said, fishing a tin cookie box out of a kitchen drawer, "now that the grannies are gone, anybody want some weed?"

"You know I do," Mick said.

"And you know I don't," Jack said just as decisively. "Can't get myself too muzzy-headed. I could get a farm call in five hours."

Honey laughed. "Well, you could never smoke nohow. The one time I did manage to get you stoned, you kept getting up to look out the window, to see if there was cops outside."

Jack laughed along with her. "Dyke or not, I guess I'm pretty much a law-abiding citizen."

Honey took out a packet of rainbow-striped rolling papers. "These are so cool. Mick found 'em up in Chattanooga." She folded a tissue-thin paper in half and began distributing pinches of green flakes across its length. "How 'bout you, Lily? Can I offer you some homegrown hospitality?"

"Not tonight, thanks. I think I'll just stick to beer." Lily had liked pot back in college; it was arguable that she had liked it too much. And now, when Honey offered it, she felt a tug of temptation to surrender to the weed's friendly, familiar oblivion. But with the trial coming up, there was no way she was going to have the dregs of an illegal drug floating around in her system. What if the Maycombs' deranged right-wing lawyer ordered her to take a drug test as evidence of her debauched lifestyle? Any risk that might cost her Mimi was a risk not worth taking.

Getting stoned, as Lily remembered it at least, wasn't boring. But watching other people get stoned sure was. Mick was already the silent type, but under the influence of marijuana, she was practically a mute. The only phrase she uttered for thirty minutes after smoking the joint was, "Honey, we got any of them Chee-tos left?"

Apparently sensing that the evening was slowing down, Jack said, "Well, I reckon I've sobered up enough to drive."

"Yeah, I guess I ought to be heading home, too." Watching Mick and Honey laughing and feeding each other Chee-tos, Lily surmised that they would like to be alone together — that as soon as the company left, they'd be making a beeline for the chenille peacock-covered bed.

Honey switched back to hostess mode. "Well, Jack, I know we'll be seeing you soon, but Lily, I hope you'll be coming back, too. I'm sure this is pretty boring compared to what you're used to in the city —"

"Not at all. Actually, this is one of the most pleasant evenings I've spent in a while," Lily said, meaning it.

In the tattoo shop's gravel parking lot, Lily suddenly shouted, "Goddamn it!"

"What is it?" Jack asked. "You too drunk to drive?"

"No, I had my last beer over an hour ago. It's just that it dawned on me . . . I can't go home tonight."

"What do you mean?"

"I'm supposed to be out of town . . . on a romantic overnight trip with Ben." She had to stop to laugh. "I

153

know it sounds crazy, but what if I went back to the house and one of my nosy sisters-in-law drove by and saw the lights on? They'd know something was up."

"Hmm," Jack said. "You lead a complicated life, don't you, lady?"

"Far too complicated." Lily felt as though she might cry again.

"I'll tell you what. Spend the night at my place tonight. I've got an extra bedroom."

"I told Ben to call me here if he needed me."

"Hang on a second. I'll take care of that." Jack disappeared behind the shop, and Lily heard her holler, "If anybody calls here for Lily, give 'em my number. She's going home with me." There was a pause, and then Jack hollered, "Not that way, you hussies!"

Chapter 14

Jack lived in an old white saltbox with a tin roof. Even in the darkness, Lily could tell that the land around it was rolling and beautiful. The sky above the farmland was sprinkled with stars.

"It's beautiful out here," Lily said, as they stood on the porch.

"Oh, yeah." Jack unlocked the front door. "There's the stars on a clear night, and on a cloudy night, there's nothin' like the sound of the rain on the roof."

The house seemed to be furnished with the same pieces Jack had grown up with. The flowered upholstery on the arms and seat of the overstuffed sofa in the living room was shiny from years of sitting, but the worn appearance of the furniture only made it more inviting.

"Your room's upstairs," Jack said, her boots clomping on the hardwood floor. "Sorry for going right off to bed, but if I get a farm call, I'll have to roll out in four hours or so."

"That's fine. I'm pretty tired." Lily followed Jack up the stairs, noting in a purely clinical fashion that Jack filled out her Levi's attractively.

Jack flipped on the light in the room at the head of the stairs — a small bedroom with floral wallpaper and an iron bed covered in a handmade quilt. A black-and-white cat who was curled up on the bed lifted his head and squinted at them irritably. "That's Hank," Jack explained. "This is kinda his bed, so he may want to share it with you. I've got two house cats, Hank here and Patsy, who sleeps with me." She smiled, a little shyly, Lily thought. "Well, you make yourself comfortable. The bathroom's next door, and there's towels in the hall closet if you need 'em."

"Thanks."

Jack studied the floor sheepishly. "If I have to get up for a farm call in the mornin', I'll just let you sleep. Feel free to let yourself out if you wake up before I get back. If I don't get called to work, though, maybe we can have breakfast, and I can show you around the place, introduce you to the animals. Sandy used to call this the Island of Misfit Critters."

Lily laughed. "About half the time, I feel like kind of a misfit critter myself."

Jack grinned. "I know what you mean. Well . . . 'night."

"Good night."

Lily undressed, crawled under the quilt, and, for the first time in a long time, fell right asleep.

She awoke to a gentle knocking on the bedroom door. Despite the fact that she wasn't sure where she was, she called, "Come in."

Jack entered carrying a tray. Lily couldn't see what was on it, but she smelled the coffee, and the aroma of caffeine was enough to make her sit up. "Good morning," she said.

"It sure is," Jack replied. "Nobody called, so I got to sleep in."

Lily glanced at the Timex on the nightstand and saw it was eight-fifteen. Since when was sleeping till eight o'clock "sleeping in"?

"I hope you don't mind me bringing you breakfast." Jack set the tray down before Lily.

Lily surveyed the spread: hot coffee, toast with butter and honey, and a blue bowl filled with sliced Georgia peaches. "It's lovely, Jack. Thank you."

Jack shrugged. "I'm not much of a cook, but toast and coffee I can handle."

"Care to join me?"

"I ate about an hour ago. I'll keep you company, though."

Jack sat on the edge of the bed while Lily ate her peaches and toast and honey. The peach slices were sweet and juicy and sunny-tasting, and Lily felt almost uncomfortable eating them in bed in such close proximity to Jack. Eating peaches in bed near another woman was the closest thing Lily had had to a sensual experience in quite some time.

"Hank was still in bed with you when I got up this morning," Jack said.

"Yeah, he was good company — a much less obtrusive bedmate than Mordecai." Lily sipped the coffee, which was strong but good. "I had a cat that died about three years ago. She was fourteen years old. I loved her so much I've never been able to get another cat. I just don't think I could stand that kind of loss again."

"Hmm." Jack reached into the bowl and popped a slice of peach into her mouth. "When I have to put sick animals down — which is the hardest part of my job, believe me — I always tell the owner to go out and find another pet. They won't be able to love the new pet the same way they loved the old one, but maybe they can find a new way to love."

Lily looked into Jack's clear blue eyes and wondered if it was really pets they were talking about. "So," she said, opting to change the subject as soon as possible, "do I get a tour of the farm before I go?"

"Sure." Jack's tone lightened. "I tell you what. Let me take your tray. You get yourself cleaned up, and just knock on the door of my room when you're ready. There's clean towels in the bathroom and a new toothbrush."

After Lily made herself presentable, she entered Jack's room to find her working on a computer, which looked incongruous with the rustic farmhouse surroundings: IBM meets *American Gothic*. "Hey," Jack said, looking up at Lily. "Even horse doctors keep their records on computer, these days. Speaking of horses, I've gotta vaccinate a couple mares on Wednesday. You wanna come?"

"Sure. I've not gotten to sketch any horses yet."

Jack turned off the computer and stood. "Okay, well, let's start the tour. This is my room."

Lily looked at the overflowing bookshelves that lined the walls. "Quite a book collection you've got here."

"One of my city girlfriends used to tease me 'cause I talk like a hick. She said as many books as I read, I oughta know better."

"I like your accent."

Jack looked down. Was she blushing? "I think the way you talk oughta tell people somethin' about you. I don't like the idea that everybody oughta sound like they're reading the nightly news."

"Me neither." Lily scanned the volumes in the nearest bookcase — they were all veterinary medicine books, with polysyllabic titles. "Not exactly light reading here."

"Nope, that bookcase is just professional stuff — boring to everybody but me." She glanced at the case across the room. "What you want's probably over there."

Lily's jaw dropped when she saw the other bookcase — six wide shelves stuffed with lesbian fiction. The books were paperbacks mostly: classics like *We Too Are Drifting*, *Beebo Brinker*, *Desert of the Heart,* and *Curious Wine*. But there were also several recent titles Lily hadn't read. "It's amazing to see so many books like this in a place . . . like this."

"Yeah. Versailles doesn't even have a bookstore, let alone a place where you can buy lesbian books. Let's just say I'm on a first-name basis with all the gals who take mail-order calls for Naiad Press. I call this bookcase the Faulkner County Lesbian Lending Library. If you wanna borrow somethin', go ahead. I don't even charge overdue fines."

"Thanks." Lily pulled a couple of mysteries off the

shelves. "Charlotte used to tease me about how many mysteries I read. She said the difference between her and me was that she read books to put them in a theoretical context, whereas I read books to find out whodunit."

Jack smiled. "I'm sure she wouldn't have thought much of my reading habits either."

Lily winced at the appropriate but still painful use of the past tense in reference to Charlotte. Jack must have noticed it, because she quickly blurted, "So, ready to see the farm?"

The morning sun shone on the green pasture and freshly painted barn, making the pastoral scene so cheerful it could have sprung to life from the pages of a Little Golden Book. Of course, in a Little Golden Book, the horse in the pasture wouldn't be quite so swaybacked.

The old chestnut gelding's spine dipped in the shape of a horseshoe. "This ole boy was treated awful mean by his owners," Jack said. "I figured the least I could do was let him get old and fat." The horse nuzzled the pocket of Jack's coveralls in search of sugar cubes. Jack fished out a cube and handed it to Lily. "Here, feed it to him. Just hold it in the flat of your palm. Not that he's got much teeth to bite you with."

Lily offered the sugar cube and scratched the horse's velvety nose.

As they walked across the farmland, they were assailed by dogs — brown dogs, black dogs, yellow dogs, and spotted dogs, all of questionable breeding but unquestionable devotion. Jack led Lily into the barn. A black streak shot past them. "That was D-Con," Jack explained. "Barn cat. Standoffish."

"Runoffish, more like," Lily said. "Thing took off so fast I wouldn't have known it was a cat if you hadn't told me."

Jack laughed. "I told you about my one-horned goat, didn't I?" She led Lily to a stall, the home of a black-and-white ram with a single, curlicued horn. Seeing company, he rested his front hooves on the fence. His eyes, like all goats' eyes, were innocent and knowing at the same time.

"Well, aren't you cute?" Lily scratched his bony back. "You might just be making a cameo appearance in my new book."

"Ole Pan here's the way I got Sandy to come to my place the first time. I told her I had a unicorn and asked her if she wanted to come see it. Pretty slick, huh?"

"Pretty slick indeed." Lily was attempting to rescue her shirttail from Pan, who was nibbling it as though it was a delicacy. She finally pulled it out of his mouth and, laughing, turned toward Jack, who was looking at her with a hard-to-read expression.

"Was Charlotte pretty?" Jack asked.

It took Lily a moment to get her bearings. "Um, yes, I thought so. She wasn't that emaciated, doe-eyed kind of pretty that you see in the magazines. Hers wasn't a fragile beauty . . . but bigger and stronger."

"Butch?"

"Yeah, I guess you could call her that. She wasn't butch in the same way that —" She started to say that "you are," but stopped herself. "In the same way that Mick is, but yeah, you could call her butch. Why do you ask?"

"I don't know. I guess I was just curious about your . . . type."

They walked out of the barn and into the sunlight. "Well, Charlotte was definitely my type." She thought of Charlotte in her various guises — in her jeans and blazer, in her motorcycle jacket, in nothing at all. "I miss her so much."

"I know you do." Jack draped a companionable arm over Lily's shoulders. "I know you do 'cause I miss Daddy. I know it's not the same thing, but I did live with him my whole life except when I was off at school. 'Course, it was easier for me. I was expecting him to go."

Lily was sobbing now. She was embarrassed to be doing it, but embarrassment wasn't enough to stop her.

"I'm sorry, Lily. I didn't mean to upset you. I just . . . you mentioned Charlotte earlier, so I thought it was okay to talk about her."

"It is okay. Sometimes, though, this wave of loss just sweeps over me."

"I know. And if I hadn't brought her up, it wouldn't have happened." She produced a clean white hanky from the pocket of her coveralls and handed it to Lily. "I want to make you feel better, not worse."

"You do make me feel better. Thanks for the tour . . . and the peaches . . . and the snot rag." She wiped her eyes. "I've gotta go, though. I've got to meet Ben so we can pick up Mimi, after our alleged overnight trip."

"Don't forget those books you left on the porch."

"Thanks." Lily retrieved the books and opened her car door. "Well . . . see ya."

"Yeah. You still wanna go see those mares this week?"

"Sure."

"Okay, I'll carry you there, then?"

Lily smiled at Jack's Southern speech. "That'd be great." Lily backed out of the driveway and watched as the receding figure of Jack stood in front of the farmhouse, watching Lily drive away.

Chapter 15

When Lily came into the living room to announce that dinner was ready, she found Jack lying on her back on the floor, holding up Mimi, whose little arms were outstretched like the wings of an airplane.

"She'll play airplane forever," Lily said. "My arms always get tired before she does."

"Not mine. If I can carry a calf, I can play airplane with a baby girl."

Lily and Mimi had gone with Jack this afternoon while she vaccinated the mares. Mimi had played in a pile of sweet-smelling hay while Lily had sketched the beautiful animals.

Lily had been planning on cooking dinner for Ben and Ken tonight, and so she had invited Jack to join them. She was making ratatouille with fresh vegetables Granny McGilly had brought them from her garden. A one-dish meal could always be stretched to feed one more person.

The only creature in the household who seemed to object to Jack's presence was Mordecai. When he saw his veterinarian walk in the door, he had slunk down the hall and hidden under Mimi's crib. Jack had lured him out with Milk-Bones and assurances that she was not there in an official capacity.

Ben and Ken were cuddling on the couch. Lily had never seen her "husband" so happy. For as long as she'd known him, Ben had a cynical streak that was equally likely to express itself in dark humor or sulkiness. Since Ken had arrived on the scene, Ben's sulkiness had disappeared entirely.

Lily, Jack, Ben, and Ken sat companionably around the dinner table. For a moment it reminded Lily of her and Ben's old days with Dez and Charlotte, except that Ken lacked Dez's flamboyance, and Jack . . . Jack was not Charlotte.

After dinner, Ben announced that he and Ken were going back to Ken's place for dessert.

Lily grinned as she cleared the dinner dishes. "I bet I know what's on the dessert menu."

Jack laughed. "Not been married half a year, Lily, and he's already stepping out on you."

Ben's face reddened, but he was laughing.

"You just be sure not to fall asleep over there,"

Lily warned. "You need to be spending the night at home, like a dutiful husband."

"Don't worry. I won't neglect my husbandly duties."

With Ben and Ken gone and Mimi tucked into bed, Lily and Jack sat together on the couch, coffee in hand.

"Mimi's a sweet little thing." Jack paused to sip her coffee. "Fun to play with."

"Well, thanks for wearing her down. She went out as soon as her head hit the pillow."

"I like kids. I reckon if I hadn't been a vet, I woulda been a pediatrician. Of course, I wanted kids to like me, and no kid ever likes going to the doctor."

Lily sipped her coffee. "Did you ever think about having kids of your own?"

Jack grinned. "I thought about it before. I could actually picture myself changing diapers and heating bottles, but there was no way in hell I could picture myself pregnant."

Lily laughed. "A pregnant butch is a sight to behold. You should've seen Charlotte. Once she started to show, she went to Kmart and bought a bunch of oversized T-shirts and drawstring sweatpants. She said there was no way in hell she was putting on a maternity dress."

"I don't blame her. So how come she was the one that ended up carrying the baby?"

"We determined it very scientifically. We drew names out of a hat. So I could just as easily have been Mimi's biological mother instead of Charlotte, and Ben could have been Mimi's biological dad instead of Dez."

"Have you ever thought how much easier your life would be now if things had turned out that way?"

"Many times. Of course, if Ben and I had been the parents, we would've had a different little girl than the one we have. And I wouldn't trade Mimi for anything." Lily set down her coffee cup. "God, the closer the hearing gets, the more nervous I get. I'm afraid to say I'll be glad when it's over, though, because I'll only be glad if everything turns out okay."

"I know." Jack took Lily's hand in hers.

Lily's first instinct was to pull away, but the strength in Jack's big, gentle hand was comforting.

"I also feel bad about lying all the time," Lily said. "I've never been so dishonest before. I spend so much of my time just hoping I'm doing the right thing."

Jack looked down at Lily's hand in hers. "I'll tell you what, Lily. It's wrong that anybody would try to take Mimi away from you. It's so wrong, that anything you do to get to keep her is the right thing."

"Thank you for saying that. I've wondered what you think of me for doing this. You're a good friend, Jack. I'm glad I met you."

"I'm glad I met you, too." Jack was silent for a moment, looking down at Lily's hand. "It's been real lonely around the house with Daddy gone, and the past few years I've ended up being the bachelor friend to all my friends in couples, and then —" She cut herself off. "I'm sorry. I'm doing a bad job of saying this."

Lily pulled her hand away. "Of saying what?"

Jack half grinned. "See? I told you I was doing a bad job." She looked down, and her voice became serious again. "I guess what I'm trying to say is . . .

oh, hell." Jack looked up at Lily and reached out to push Lily's hair out of her face. Lily watched passively as Jack leaned toward her and softly touched her lips to hers. Lily was paralyzed.

As soon as Jack pulled away, Lily scooted to the opposite end of the couch. She hadn't felt another woman's lips on hers since Charlotte's, and the feel of Jack's lips made her ache for Charlotte's kisses. But there was something else, too. "Jack, I'm not ready . . ."

"I know. I ought not to have done that. It was just that I couldn't make the words come out right, and I've always been better at doing things than saying em. I know you're not ready yet, Lily. You're a widow in mourning — I understand that. I guess what I'm trying to say is . . . if you ever decide you're ready, then I'm ready, too."

Lily's head felt as if it might explode from being so full of fear and sadness and confusion. She hadn't even been allowed a decent period of mourning before she had to worry about losing her daughter. Then there were the numerous pressures of maintaining a fake marriage, the hearing that was coming up sooner than she liked to think about, and now this. "Jack, I can't even think about this right now. I still love Charlotte —"

"And you always will. I understand that. But I don't think Charlotte would want you to spend the rest of your life alone . . . to bury yourself right along with her. Once the hearing is over, Lily, you're gonna have to take a little of the time you've been using to think about Mimi's needs and think about your own."

Lily choked back a sob. "Once the hearing is over, I might not have my daughter."

"That's true. But even if you don't, you don't have to be all alone."

"Well, thank you for saying that. You're —"

"A good friend? I know. And if that's all I can be now, I accept that. I just had to let you know, Lily. I had to tell you because the other mornin', when I woke up knowing you were in my house ... the house was a lot happier place because you were in it."

Lily's emotions were scattered all over the place. She felt simultaneously trapped, terrified, and touched.

Jack rose from the couch. "I know you're not in a position to make any promises, Lily. I just wanted to say my piece, and I reckon I've said it."

"Yeah, I guess you have."

"There's just one more thing, though. I wanna make sure this isn't my imagination. When our eyes meet, when you look at me ... there's somethin' there, isn't there?"

Lily thought of the first time she saw Jack — the moment she realized Jack was a woman. She thought of Jack's hands working to heal a wounded animal, of Jack rolling on the floor playing with Mimi. As much as she'd like to, there was no denying it. "Yeah," she said, avoiding eye contact. "There's something there."

Jack flashed a wide grin. "I didn't think it was my imagination. I guess that was all I really wanted to know." She headed toward the door. "I'm sorry if I made you uncomfortable. I'll go now."

Lily knew that Jack wanted her to tell her to stay. But Lily was ready for Jack to leave. She had reached emotional overload, and all she could think about was curling up in a fetal ball in the womb of her bed. "Good night, Jack."

"Good night."

In her bed, Lily cried because Charlotte had died before Lily had finished loving her. She cried because she knew that if Charlotte had died at the age of eighty, she still would have died before Lily had finished loving her. She cried because of the choice that lay before her: to stay married to a memory, or to move on.

Rationally, Lily knew that Jack had a point — that Charlotte would have wanted Lily's life to go on. But the problem was that Lily wasn't sure she wanted her life to go on. Life seemed like a dangerous contact sport, full of opportunities for loss and injury, with victory being only the dimmest of possibilities. Right now, Lily wasn't sure she even felt like being a spectator of such a sport, let alone a player.

Chapter 16

Lily rarely drank beer before noon. As a matter of fact, this was probably the first time she'd drunk a beer before two P.M. in her life. But today was a special occasion — in the same sense that the day you're scheduled to get a much-dreaded pap smear is a special occasion.

The hearing was two weeks from today, and yesterday she, Ben, and Buzz Dobson had sat down to plan their strategy. Buzz, once again, had turned his meager thoughts to the subject of Lily's appearance.

"I was thinking, Lily," he'd said, biting into a

sloppy hamburger that squirted ketchup all over his shirt. "It'd probably be a good idea to go ahead and pay some attention to your appearance. Get a nice hairdo, buy yourself two or three pretty dresses, go around for a couple weeks before the trial looking . . . looking —"

"Normal?" Lily had offered helpfully.

"Well, I wasn't gonna put it that way, but yeah. You know, just let people see you out with Mimi at the playground, at church maybe, looking the way people around here expect a young mother to look."

So yesterday afternoon Lily had grudgingly called Sheila and asked what beauty shop she and Tracee would recommend. If any women embodied "the way people around here expect a young mother to look," they were Sheila and Tracee.

Sheila had been hysterical with joy at Lily's call, sure, Lily thought, that the Faulkner County chapter of the Stepford Wives had just recruited a new member. "Ooh, me and Tracee already have an appointment over at the Chatterbox for tomorrow at eleven-thirty," she'd squealed. "I'm sure they wouldn't mind if you tagged along. Oh, it'll be so much fun! We can get our hair done and get facials, and you can even get a Mary Kay makeover if you want. Me and Tracee won't, though, 'cause we don't *need* a makeover. And I heard they got some new dresses over at the La-Di-Da. Maybe we could walk over there after we get our hair fixed, and spend some of the McGilly boys' money."

And so here Lily sat, swilling beer in the morning, waiting for Sheila and Tracee to come get her. If Ben hadn't already taken Mimi to Jeanie's, she'd be tempted to grab her daughter and flee, before the peroxided pod people could turn her into one of them. She disposed of the empty beer bottle and went to the bathroom to brush her teeth. Just as she was spitting, she heard the horn of Sheila's Lexus.

Lily had hoped that the stylist at the Chatterbox would be a gay man — a Faulkner County queen who, out of allegiance to his family, had chosen to live and work in Versailles. Lily had no such luck. Instead, the Chatterbox was run by a creature who called itself Doreen and who worked with the theory that one could make more money in the beauty industry by undermining the self-esteem of one's customers.

When Sheila and Tracee presented Lily to Doreen, she shook her head and mumbled, "My, my, my. Look what the cat drug in."

Not that Doreen looked that hot herself. Her straw-textured hair was dyed neon orange, and her eyelids were shadowed with bright turquoise. But the most fascinating thing about Doreen was her eyebrows — or her simulated eyebrows.

The old lady (how old was impossible to tell beneath the layers of pancake makeup) had plucked or shaved her naturally occurring brows and painted on violent black slashes that began at the bridge of her nose and ended up at her hairline above her temples. If this was the woman who was in charge of her makeover, Lily thought she was more likely to end up looking like an extra from *Star Trek* than an ordinary wife and mother.

Doreen turned Sheila and Tracee over to her assistant for their trims and root touch-ups. She looked at Lily, stubbed out her cigarette, and said to no one in particular, "Well, I reckon I'll have to roll up my sleeves to deal with this one." When she finally addressed Lily directly, she ordered, "Sit down, honey. And get comfortable. This is gonna take a while."

Lily tried to sit still while Doreen yanked on her hair. "Never seen so many rat nests in my life," Doreen muttered, her cigarette clenched between her teeth. Lily was fairly sure she felt a few ashes drop on her head.

She knew her hair was a mess. She hadn't done anything to it except wash it since Charlotte died, and her once-funky white-girl braids had turned into mats and tangles. Doreen pulled and combed so hard that Lily was sure her hair was being torn out by its roots. Tattoos and body piercings were painless compared to this torture.

"Well, I reckon I got it combed out enough to wash it anyway," Doreen said finally. When Lily turned her head to look in the mirror, she was greeted by the image of Elsa Lanchester in *Bride of Frankenstein*.

"Lord, girl, don't look at it yet. We ain't even halfway there. It's a good thing I eat my Wheaties this mornin'." She tucked a towel into the collar of Lily's plastic smock. "Lean back in the chair now."

After Doreen scrubbed Lily's scalp as though it needed de-lousing, Lily sat up again. Doreen fluffed her hair with her red talons. "We're gonna hafta take a lotta this length off," she muttered. "You got split ends on top of your split ends." Doreen's scissors began snip-snip-snipping in a seemingly random pattern, and Lily sucked in her breath as large hunks of hair fell onto her smock and the floor.

"How's it going?" Sheila asked brightly. She and Tracee stood together, their coiffures trimmed and touched up.

Doreen looked Lily over and frowned. "It'll be another hour at least."

"Hmm," Tracee said, "Well, I guess we'll go grab some lunch at the Bucket. We'll be back directly."

Doreen snipped until Lily figured she'd run out of hair, then mixed up a plastic bottle of some vile-smelling chemical solution and squeezed it on Lily's hair. Lily's eyes teared, and her nose ran. She had always drawn the body-piercing line at below-the-belt piercings, but right now a labia piercing seemed a comparative piece of cake.

"All right, back in the sink," Doreen barked like a cosmetology drill sergeant. Lily pondered the analogy as Doreen rinsed the chemicals from her hair. Just like a drill sergeant, Doreen was stamping out Lily's rebelliousness and taking away her individuality to make her an acceptable member of a team.

Hair — its color, length, and style — was always tied to individuality. After all, what was the first thing the army did to new male recruits? They gave them identical haircuts.

Lily reflected on the symbolic significance of hair as her own shortened tresses were blown dry, hot rolled, brushed, sprayed, and spritzed. When Doreen finally turned the chair to face the mirror, Lily gasped. Doreen bared her yellowed teeth in a grin, mistaking her client's shock for delight.

Lily's new short hair was not the carefree crop of a dyke. Her ashy tresses had been highlighted a sunny blonde and were now pouffed on top of her head, coming down in perfectly arranged petals around her face. It was a soccer mom's haircut — short, sassy, and sprayed so stiff that neither rain nor sleet nor storm nor hail could budge it.

Lily patted her stiff bubble of hair. With a do like this, she could be perkily reporting the six o'clock news. It was the perfect style for the image she needed to project, but looking at it still made her want to cry.

"Is that what you wanted, honey?" Doreen asked, firing up another cigarette.

"Yeah, it's perfect."

"Now I don't know if Sheila and Tracee told you or not, but I am a licensed Mary Kay consultant, so if you wanted some more makeup to complete your new look —"

"Sure. Why not?" Lily looked at Doreen's horrifying Kabuki mask of cosmetics. "But let's keep it light and natural, okay?"

"Sure, hon."

Lily's "light and natural" makeover took thirty-five minutes. Sheila and Tracee returned from their lunch break and watched Lily's transformation, oohing and ahhing as if they were watching the ceiling of the Sistine Chapel being painted.

When Lily saw herself in the mirror, her newly painted mouth formed an "O" of surprise, making her look not unlike one of those blond, blow-up sex-toy dolls. She would almost have preferred to be wearing Doreen's Kabuki mask — at least it had a spooky, avant-garde quality. As it was, her cheeks were dusted with peachy blush, her lips painted with equally peachy lipstick, her lashes brushed with mascara to give her a wide-eyed, Mary Pickford appearance. She looked — she shuddered at the word — *wholesome.*

"Doreen, you are a miracle worker!" Sheila squealed. "Come on, Lily, let's go buy you some new dresses!"

A better name for the La-Di-Da Dress Shop might be Designed-to-Be-Dowdy, Lily thought, as she scanned through the racks. All the dresses were in the prim shirtwaist style preferred by Sunday school teachers and small-town librarians. Finally, deciding all the garments were equally vile, Lily closed her eyes and pulled two dresses off the "size eight" rack at random.

The oversolicitous saleslady went into paroxysms of joy. "Oh," she crowed, "those are positively the real you!"

"Give it a rest, lady," Lily muttered, marching toward the dressing rooms. "You wouldn't know the real me if I bit you on the ass!"

"Lil-*ee!*" Tracee chided her. "You're aw-*full!*"

But she had already shut the dressing room door behind her.

In her light blue shirtwaist dress, black Naturalizer flats, and stockings, Lily was totally unrecognizable, even to herself. She was reminded of the scene in the movie *Tootsie* in which Dustin Hoffman first appears in full, dowdy drag.

When Lily went to relieve Jeanie of her babysitting duties, Mimi screamed at the sight of her. The little girl eyed Lily suspiciously, then broke down in tears. "Where's Mama? Where's Mama?" she wailed hysterically.

"Mimi-saurus, it's me. I'm your mama."

"No! Not Mama!" Mimi screamed.

"Honey, of course it's your mama," Jeanie said. "She just went to the beauty shop. Don't she look pretty?"

"Not Mama!" Mimi shrieked louder.

Lily had to carry Mimi to the bathroom and show her her tattoos in order to convince the little girl that the pristinely dressed, carefully coiffed creature before her was indeed her mother.

When Lily returned to the place she and Ben grudgingly called home, Ben took one look at her and cried, "Shit! Shiiit. Shi-it."

Lily flopped down on the sofa. "Hey, now, no profanity in front of the baby."

Ben shook his head like a wet dog. "Good god, you look like the president of the Junior League, and you say things like 'no profanity in front of the baby.' It's like you've turned into a . . . a . . ."

Lily put on a mock Cockney accent. "A real lay-dee? Just call me Eliza, Professor Higgins." She kicked off her shoes and began unceremoniously peeling off her pantyhose. "We got any beer?"

Mordecai emerged from the hall and eyed Lily suspiciously. He approached her, sniffed her, and, satisfied as to her identity, settled down for an ear-scratching. Ben backed out of the room, still fixated on Lily's transformed appearance. "I'll . . . I'll get you one."

"Thanks," she said. "You're a good husband."

Ben returned with their beers and sat down on the couch. "Say, why don't I drive over to Callahan and pick us up a pizza for dinner? You can't be in the kitchen cooking, looking like that. You'll feel like fucking Harriet Nelson."

Mimi looked up from her shape sorter and joyously exclaimed, "Fuckin'!"

"Mimi, that's a grown-up word." Lily leaned back on the couch and sucked down some beer. "A lot of good it's gonna do me to change my entire image if my daughter's gonna have the vocabulary of a long-shoreman."

"Don't worry; she won't have to testify." Ben flipped through the Versailles/Callahan phone book. Ripping that phone book would be no feat of strength, Lily thought. Mimi could probably do it.

"So . . ." Ben said, "mushroom, green pepper, and black olive?"

"Sure." Lily was astonished at the tiredness in her voice.

After Ben went to fetch the pizza, Lily made a bowl of oatmeal and a slice of toast for Mimi, whose idea of good eating was breakfast three times a day. Lily tied on Mimi's bib, sat down with her, and began to spoon the warm cereal into the little girl's mouth.

"No, Mama," Mimi said. "Feed self."

"Well, okay, grown-up girl." She handed the spoon over, and Mimi took it into her tiny fist. Mimi shoveled away, managing to convey about sixty percent of the food into her mouth. Overall, she was doing a better job than Buzz Dobson.

Every day Mimi was getting more independent, learning to do more things for herself, adding more words to her vocabulary, including some she'd be better off without. Colorful vocabulary or not, Lily was proud of Mimi, and she loved watching her grow and learn. She thought of the other steps Mimi would be taking in the next year or so — moving from a crib to a bed, learning to use the potty — and hoped she would be there to help her daughter with these difficult milestones.

Mimi reached a dimpled, oatmeal-gooey hand out to touch Lily's stiff hair. "Funny Mama."

Lily had to agree. "Yeah, I'm pretty funny looking all right. Are you done with your dinner?"

"All done."

"Okay, let's go hose you off, then."

Mimi grinned, flashing her perfect, white baby teeth. "Baffy?"

"That's right. Bathy time."

As Lily watched Mimi splash happily in the tub, she found herself wondering what the Maycombs and their kind thought she would do to damage her daughter. Did they think she was simply raising Mimi to recruit her, to train her from the earliest possible age in the rites of Sappho? Such thinking — if it could even be called thinking — was ridiculous. As long as Mimi found someone who'd be good to her, Lily didn't care whom she grew up to love, male or female. She and Charlotte had decided to have a child to love, not to recruit.

It was the fundamentalists who recruited. From the time their children were babies, they dragged them to Sunday school and church for hours on end, indoctrinating them when they were too young to know what hit them. Maybe this was why fundamentalists always assumed gays and lesbians were raising their children with some kind of agenda in mind; the fundamentalists themselves certainly were.

Lily loved the way Mimi smelled and felt when she was fresh out of the tub. After she got Mimi diapered and dressed, Lily sat down in the nursery's rocking chair for storytime. Mimi toddled over to her bookshelf. Lily was amused to note that while three of her own picture books were on the shelf, Mimi always avoided them like the plague. Everybody was a critic.

Mimi returned to the rocking chair with Janell Cannon's beautifully illustrated book *Stellaluna*. Lily cuddled her daughter on her lap, opened the book, and began to read.

Stellaluna was the story of a baby fruit bat who gets separated from her mother and so is raised, for a time, by a family of birds. The birds are kind to Stellaluna as long as she exhibits birdlike behavior. She is not allowed to fly at night or hang upside down, and she is fed insects instead of the mangoes she loves. While Stellaluna appreciates the birds' kindness, she is only happy when she is reunited with her fruit bat family.

Lily's eyes filled as she read the book to Mimi. It was amazing how a simple children's book could say so much. She identified with Stellaluna. A lost fruit bat, she was taken in by the McGillys. Their kindness was unquestionable, but it was contingent on her pretending to be something she was not. The McGillys were her bird family — well-meaning, but different from her — and capable of offering her only insects, not the mangoes she craved.

She tucked Mimi into her crib just as Ben returned with the pizza. After they ate, Lily asked, "So are you just gonna hang out here tonight?"

"Thought I would. Ken has some god-awful departmental function tonight."

"So . . . would it be okay if I went out for a while?"

"Sure. I'll look after Mimi if she wakes up."

Lily was up from the table already.

"So where are you going?" Ben asked.

"I'm going out . . . to get some mangoes."

"What do you mean, mangoes? You can't buy mangoes in Faulkner County."

Lily grabbed her car keys and walked out the door

without bothering to explain. There might be no mangoes in Faulkner County, but she did remember something from her breakfast with Jack. Like a mango, it was sweet, juicy, and succulent. There were no mangoes in Faulkner County, but there were peaches.

Chapter 17

Jack opened the door of her farmhouse and surveyed the new, prim Lily. "Isn't it kinda late for Jehovah's Witnesses?"

"Jack, it's me."

"Lily? Omigod, what happened to you?"

"The Chatterbox beauty shop happened to me. Can I come in?"

Still slack-jawed, Jack backed away from the door so Lily could enter.

Once the door closed behind her, words started spilling from Lily's lips faster than she could control them. "I don't even know why I came here, really. I just feel so . . . weird. Before all this shit happened, my outside always matched my inside, but now nothing matches. Buzz Dobson told me it would improve my chances with the judge if I tried to look respectable, and now when I look at myself in the mirror I don't even see me anymore."

She didn't realize she was crying until Jack offered her a handkerchief. "I'm scared, Jack. I'm scared of losing Mimi, and I'm scared of losing myself. What if my insides change to match what's on the outside, Jack? What if I pretend to be a bird for so long that I forget I'm a fruit bat?"

Jack's brow knitted. "A fruit bat?"

"It's just a metaphor."

"Come here." Jack pulled her close in a tight, warm hug. "You're still you, Lily. You're just wearing a costume. Think of it as Halloween in July."

Lily buried her face in the collar of Jack's soft coveralls. They smelled of sweet hay and horse flesh. "I need to be reminded of who I am by someone who understands, by someone who's . . ."

"A fruit bat?"

Lily smiled. "Yeah."

"Lily, what I said the other night . . . I know I did a bad job of saying it, but I still meant it. I know you still love Charlotte — that you always will love her, but where she is right now, she can't help you. And since she can't, I'd like to be the person who does, who looks after you, helps you with Mimi, gives you the love I know you've been missing. I'd like to be that person. Even if it's just for right now, I'd like to be that person."

Lily looked at Jack — her broad shoulders, her strong, square jaw, and her clear blue eyes. Looking at Jack, Lily felt kindness and kinship, but she also felt something else — a stirring she hadn't felt since her wedding night when she had dreamed of Charlotte. Standing on tiptoe in her frumpy, Sunday school-teacher shoes, Lily kissed Jack on the lips, resting one hand on the back of Jack's head to feel the velvety stubble of her close-cropped hair.

"Wow," Jack said, when they broke apart. "That wasn't a pity kiss, was it?"

"I don't do pity kisses."

"Good." Jack leaned down and kissed Lily this time. It was a long kiss. Their lips were parted and locked, and Lily pressed her body against Jack's.

Lily's mind was protesting, but her body was telling her mind to shut the hell up. It had been so long since she had felt such closeness, and she needed it — needed the comfort of two bodies twined together, needed to be in the one situation where there was no denying what she was. When the kiss ended, Lily was gasping for breath.

"The way I see it," Jack said, wiping some of Lily's Mary Kay lipstick from her mouth, "we've got two options. I can make us a pot of coffee and we can sit in the kitchen and pretend like nothing happened. Or we can go upstairs." She looked Lily square in the eye. "It's your call."

Lily was tired of pretending. "Upstairs," she said, barely above a whisper.

Jack grinned. "Good choice. Put your arms around my neck."

Lily did as she was told and whooped with surprise

as Jack lifted her up in her arms. "What is this, a little Rhett-and-Scarlett action?" Lily laughed. "You'd better put me down. You're gonna break your back."

"Nah," Jack said. "You weigh less than that damn dog of yours."

Jack carried Lily up the stairs and dropped her on the bed. Patsy the cat, who had been snoozing on the quilt by the footboard, leaped from the bed and stalked off, offended.

Jack laughed. "It's been a long time since I've had a reason to kick ole Patsy outta bed." She looked down at Lily as she lay on the bed, and Lily felt her eyes on her almost as if they were hands. "So beautiful."

"Thank you."

"And I even kinda like that dress. You know, I used to have a bad crush on my Sunday school teacher." Jack sat on the side of the bed and pulled off her cowboy boots, then leaned over Lily and kissed her.

It had been so long since Lily had felt the weight of another woman on her, another body pressing into her own. Without even thinking, she wrapped her right leg around Jack's waist.

"Mmm," Jack purred. "Let me help you with that dress." Slowly, methodically, Jack undid each button from calf to waist, then from neckline to waist. When Lily's underwear had been cast aside, Jack said "beautiful" and leaned over her.

"Wait." Lily had become suddenly aware that Jack was still wearing her coveralls, looking more like she was about to deliver a calf than make love. "Aren't you gonna undress?"

"Oh, I forgot." Jack stood up and unceremoniously

shucked off her coveralls. She looked self-conscious for a moment, standing there in a white tank undershirt and a pair of plain white briefs. "The shirt, too?" she asked.

"Uh-huh."

Jack pulled off the undershirt and stood before Lily, all rippling biceps and strong thighs. Her breasts were small and high, and her stomach was tautly muscled — not from the machines at a gym, but from hard work. "Wow," Lily sighed.

"Ah, nothin' special." Jack's freckled cheeks reddened — adorably, Lily thought.

"Are you kidding, woman? If you lived in Atlanta, you'd have to beat the dykes off with a softball bat. Come here."

Lily shuddered as Jack's skin met her own. Jack was a strong lover, skillful yet passionate. Her hands were everywhere, on Lily's breasts, belly, thighs, stroking so many surfaces that Lily wondered if Jack had a couple of extra pairs of hands she kept hidden from view.

When Jack entered Lily, she took her quickly to orgasm, then waited inside her a few moments, and took her again. Lily clutched the headboard and bit the pillow to stop the scream that she felt building up in her throat. After her third climax, she gasped, "We're gonna have to take it easy a minute. I think I'm losing brain cells here."

Jack slowly withdrew her hand. "Well, why don't we try this instead?" Jack threw the quilt over Lily's naked body and burrowed under it until her head was between Lily's thighs. Lily closed her eyes and sighed. For the first time since Charlotte's death, her mind was clear and empty, and she gave herself over to pleasure. Her orgasm was beautiful and shattering, and tension drained from her eyes in the form of tears.

As Lily lay exhausted in Jack's arms, she said, "Your turn."

"Huh?"

"Your turn. You did me; now I do you."

"You don't have to if you don't want to. A lotta girls, I wear 'em out so bad, they pass right out."

Lily smiled at Jack's cockiness and slid on top of her. "Not this girl." She pressed her lips to Jack's and let her hands trail down her lean, muscular body.

As they lay holding each other, Jack said, "I wish you could stay the night. I'd make you breakfast again."

"Peaches and coffee?"

"Mm-hm."

"I'd love to stay, but you know I can't."

Jack grinned. "Gosh, you don't think your husband suspects you're a dyke, do you?"

Lily laughed. "I'd better get dressed." She rose and walked across the room to retrieve her underwear. "How did my panties end up all the way over here?"

"Beats me." Jack watched her dress. "Any chance we could maybe do this again?"

Lily buttoned her dress. "Well, I'm not in a position right now to make any promises, but yeah, I think maybe we could."

Jack pulled on her underwear. "You know, don't you, that I don't just do this with any girl. I used to, but I don't do it anymore unless it means something."

"I know." Lily looked at Jack, vulnerable in her underwear. She felt like she should say something else, but she couldn't find the words.

Jack zipped up her coveralls. "I'll walk you to the door."

Downstairs, they kissed good night in the same place where earlier kisses had begun their evening. "Wait. Don't go yet." Jack disappeared into the kitchen for a moment. When she came back, she pressed something soft and round into Lily's hand. "Eat it when you wake up in the morning, and think about me."

In her car, in the dark, Lily stroked the soft skin of the peach and smiled.

Chapter 18

The hearing was tomorrow. Lily couldn't sit still
for a second. She paced around the house like a caged
panther, rehearsing the lines she and Buzz Dobson
had gone over, making sure her outfit for the next day
wasn't wrinkled. She felt like an actress preparing for
opening night of a play, except that if the play
bombed, her life and her daughter's life would be permanently damaged.

Even Ben, who had been discounting all of Lily's
fears about the hearing, was showing signs of
nervousness. He kept riffling through the suits and

ties in his closet. If he was going to try to pass himself off as heterosexual, he couldn't be too well dressed.

Granny McGilly had taken Mimi out for a few hours this afternoon, on the theory that Ben and Lily needed some grown-up time to collect themselves. Granny McGilly also wanted Mimi to get used to spending time with her, since she was serving as babysitter during the hearing.

For their grown-up time, Lily and Ben had invited Jack and Ken to come over — to comfort them in their time of hysteria. At first Lily had been wary about inviting the two of them over so much, but Ben assured her she had nothing to fear: In Faulkner County, the rumor was that Lily and Ben were playing matchmaker for the bachelor professor and old-maid veterinarian. Once again, Lily found herself marveling at the obliviousness of straight people.

As they waited for Ken and Jack to arrive, Ben sat on the couch and Lily paced the length of the living room. "Could you just light for a minute?" Ben asked. "I feel like I'm living with a giant hummingbird."

Lily forced herself to sit in the armchair. Her knees bent, but her body didn't relax. "We were insane to think we could pull this off. We should've stayed in Atlanta and fought this honestly."

"I still like our chances here. And besides, if we hadn't come back to Versailles, I never would've run into Ken, and you never would've met Jack. Who'd have thought a sham marriage would put us in a situation where we'd both fall in love?"

"Hey, *you* fell in love, buddy. I've never said anything about being in love."

Ben rolled his eyes. "Well, no, you've never said

191

anything, but I have a sneaking suspicion that you and Dr. Jack have been doing more than trotting off to farms and giving pigs enemas." He leaned forward. "I saw your face when you came home the other night, Mrs. McGilly. I know the face of an adulterous wife when I see one."

Lily smiled and shook her head. Jack had been a comfort to her since the moment she met her — a remarkable friend and, as of the other night, a remarkable bedmate. But she couldn't just pretend the years she had with Charlotte didn't exist, couldn't just climb up the ladder and dive into another relationship . . . not so soon. "I still love Charlotte, Ben."

"Of course you do. And I never stopped loving Dez. Even after we weren't lovers anymore, I still loved him. And now that he's dead, I still love him. I don't have to stop loving Dez just because I love Ken. And you don't have to stop loving Charlotte just because you love Jack."

Before Lily could form a response, the doorbell rang. She rose to answer it, eager to escape the conversation, and let in Ken, who was carrying a large white shopping bag, and Jack, who was carrying a small brown paper sack.

"Okay," Ken said, unpacking his bag on the coffee table. "We have two bottles of champagne, artichoke dip with sliced baguette, smoked salmon with crackers, and fresh fruit with poppy seed dressing."

"And paper napkins and a bag of potato chips." Jack grinned. "My elegant contribution."

When Ken popped the cork of the champagne bottle, Mordecai fled the room in terror. It was nice to have something to laugh at.

"Shouldn't we have the champagne after the hearing?" Lily asked. "If we win?"

"Well, I thought about that," Ken said. "But I figured you'd need it more before the hearing."

The two couples fed each other dainty bits of food and drained the first bottle of champagne far faster than was probably good for them. By the time they were halfway through the second bottle, Ben and Ken were necking on the couch, and Lily was sitting on Jack's lap in the armchair.

"Well, I guess we know why the French are supposed to be so sexy," Lily laughed, watching Ben and Ken kiss. "It's the champagne."

Ben and Ken broke apart. "Sorry," Ken laughed, "champagne always has that effect on me."

"I'm not complaining." Ben's face was flushed.

Lily knew that Ben had loved Dez, but by the time she met them, they were acting like a bickering old married couple. Seeing Ben with Ken was completely different. In Ken's presence, Ben seemed lighthearted and light-headed, giddy with excitement. Lily wondered if that's what Ben was like in the early days of his relationship with Dez. Or was each love different?

"The champagne's got nothing to do with it," Jack teased. "It's you city people coming down here and corrupting the likes of Ken and me. I mean, look at this living room . . . the empty champagne bottles, the kissing boys . . . we're practically having an orgy here!"

Ben and Ken were too busy kissing to respond to Jack's comment, but Lily laughed. "Why don't you boys get a room? Like, Ben's room, for instance?"

Ken turned to Ben. "What do you say?"

Ben reddened and drained his champagne glass.

"Sure. Why not?" Laughing, they strolled down the hall, hand in hand.

Jack took Lily's empty glass. "More champagne, milady?"

"Well, it's a shame to let it go to waste."

Jack refilled their glasses and motioned for Lily to join her on the couch. They linked their arms and tried to drink champagne out of each other's glasses, but the alcohol made them clumsy and Jack spilled some of the golden liquid on Lily. They laughed, and then Jack took Lily's glass and set it down on the coffee table.

"Can't stand to see that champagne go to waste," Jack said, leaning over and licking the spilled drops off Lily's collarbone. Lily gasped with delight. "You know what?" Jack whispered in her ear. "I've never seen your bedroom."

Lily giggled in spite of herself. "You really want to? With the boys just across the hall?"

"They're busy. They won't pay any attention to us. And we'll be quiet." She smiled. "Not like last time."

In Lily's room, inhibitions washed away by the champagne, Jack and Lily undressed each other and slid into a slow, sensual round of lovemaking. The first time they made love, it had been with the ravenous urgency of a starving person sitting down to a lavish meal. Today, though, with the whole afternoon ahead of them, they savored the experience, enjoying the taste of each other's kisses, exploring the texture of each other's skin, and breathing low sighs of pleasure.

Between the champagne and Jack's capable hands, Lily felt the coils of tension she had been carrying for the past week start to unwind. Ever since she had come to Versailles, Lily had been trying to control a situation that seemed uncontrollable. But here, beneath Jack's hands and mouth, she could allow herself to lose control — to turn off her brain for a few minutes and surrender to sensuality.

Afterward, as they lay naked beneath the cool sheets, Lily said, "Have you ever heard the expression that you grow a new heart for every child you have?"

Jack started. "You and Ben aren't expecting, are you?"

Lily laughed. "Not unless a star is rising somewhere in the East." She laid her head on Jack's freckled shoulder. "No, I was just thinking about that idea. When I was with Charlotte, I didn't know if it would be possible for me to love anybody else . . . I just felt so full and content, you know?"

"Uh-huh."

"And then we had Mimi, and I discovered this whole other capacity for love I didn't even know I had. And then, getting to know you . . . I mean, it's not that I love Charlotte less, but with you . . . I guess sometimes meeting someone can cause you to grow a new heart, too." Lily laughed. "God, I never would've said something like that if I was sober."

"Do you mean it, though?"

Lily thought for a moment. She had spoken just then without thinking, but she had meant what she said . . . just as people usually did when they spoke without considering their words beforehand. "Yes."

"Then I'm glad you're not sober." Jack and Lily's lips met in another long, slow kiss. When they parted, there were tears in Lily's eyes.

"I'm scared, Jack."

"I know. Whatever happens, though, I'll take care of you."

Lily drifted off for a few minutes, letting herself feel almost safe in Jack's arms. When she heard the footsteps in the hall, at first she thought it was Mordecai. But then she heard the voices: "Lil-ee! Ben! You've gotta be home — the door was unlocked!"

Oh, shit. Sheila and Tracee — as always, just walking right on in whenever they felt like it.

Lily and Jack sprang out of bed and scrambled for their clothes, sure that the boys across the hall were doing the same thing. But it was no good. The bedroom door, which they hadn't closed all the way, swung open. Sheila's scream at the sight of Jack and Lily rang out at the same moment as Tracee's did when she opened the door on the boys across the hall.

"Have you never heard of knocking?" Lily yelled, pulling on her shirt.

"I always thought family didn't have to knock," Sheila said. "Of course, I thought family had nothing to hide from each other."

"Look," Ben barked, standing in the hallway wearing only his jeans, "what my wife and I choose to do in the privacy of our own home —"

"You and your 'wife' — if you can call her that — wasn't doing a thing together," Tracee interrupted. "I knew there was somethin' funny about y'all's marriage the second I laid eyes on y'all together. I said to myself, somethin' —"

"Ain't right," Sheila finished. "Oh, I wonder what Big Daddy and Mama McGilly will have to say when they realize they bought a new car and a new house for a couple of —"

"Queers!" Tracee finished for her. For two straight girls, they finished each other's sentences like an old married couple.

"Now wait just a damn minute," Jack said, towering over the two big-haired women. "I don't see why there's any reason to go off and tell Benny Jack's parents. Lily's a good mother, and if you go off blabbering like that, she could lose her daughter."

"Last thing a lezzie needs is a little girl," Sheila spat. "She's probably already been messing with her."

"Now, that's ridiculous —" Ken began.

"No," Tracee interrupted. "*This* is ridiculous. Come on, Sheila, we're taking a drive over to the big house."

And they were gone.

Jack punched the wall with the fist she had balled up while talking to Sheila and Tracee. "What do we do now?"

"Nothing to do but wait for the hammer to fall," Lily said, her voice dull and numb.

"If I know Mother and Daddy, they'll be over here within the hour. It would probably be a good idea if the two of you went home," Ben said.

"God, I feel so guilty," Ken wailed. "If I hadn't brought the champagne —"

"This still could've happened," Lily finished for him. "It's not your fault."

Jack kissed Lily's cheek. "Call me the second you know something."

Lily sighed. "I will."

Their lovers scurried off, and Lily and Ben sat on the couch, holding hands in despair. They hadn't even been to the courthouse yet, but they were already awaiting their sentence.

Chapter 19

"Well, this ain't an easy thing to talk about." Big Ben McGilly stared into his coffee mug.

Lily couldn't believe she'd had the presence of mind to brew coffee. She and Ben had sat on the couch in miserable silence for twenty minutes when she had jumped up, saying, "Well, if you're sure your parents are coming over, I might as well make some coffee."

She had thought it was insane as she was doing it, measuring out coffee just as she was about to lose her daughter and possibly her life. (After all, it wasn't inconceivable that Big Ben would arrive toting a double-barreled shotgun.) But now she saw the sense of her coffee preparation. The cups gave them all something to hold in their fidgety hands, something to stare into instead of each other's eyes.

"No, it ain't an easy thing to sit in your living room and talk about," Big Ben continued. "But I reckon ya know why we're here." He looked over at Jeanie, who looked into her coffee cup.

"Yes, sir," Lily answered, when it became clear that her husband wasn't going to say anything.

Big Ben nodded gravely. "Sheila and Tracee was over at the house a little while ago. Now why they'd be rude enough to swing a body's bedroom doors open is a mystery to me, but they told me what they seen. In no uncertain terms, you might say."

Lily looked at Ben, whose face was gray. Good god, Lily thought. He's not just upset over Mimi; he's upset because his parents are going to cut him off without a cent. Benny Jack McGilly is stunned into muteness at the thought of having to get a job. "Yes, sir," Lily said to her father-in-law, figuring that since the course of events was inevitable, she might as well speed things along.

"Now I can't say me and Jeanie was surprised by what Sheila and Tracee said they saw," Big Ben continued. "I reckon what surprised us was that y'all didn't have the presence of mind to lock the front door before ya got nekkid."

For the first time since his parents arrived, Ben looked up. "What?"

Jeanie set her cup down on the coffee table. "Why, Benny Jack, honey, we've knowed you was a homosexual since you was ten years old. And when you brought Lily home, we just kinda figgered she was one, too."

With a shaking hand, Lily set down her cup. "You . . . knew?"

Big Ben smiled. "Honey, just 'cause we live in a little-bitty town in Georgia don't mean we're stupid. Benny Jack never cared nothin' 'bout girls, and you know what they say: A tiger don't change his stripes."

"So you were going to help me keep Mimi even though you knew I was a lesbian?"

Jeanie shrugged. "Don't see why not. You're a good mama."

"And besides," Big Ben said, "I took a real dislike to them Maycombs. Never could stand people who meddle around in their grown children's affairs. After your younguns is out of your house, what they do is their bizness."

Ben was mute again, but Lily could tell it was a different kind of muteness from before — a muteness that came from the realization that in all his years, he had never given his parents enough credit for being decent, intelligent human beings.

"Well, I'm very touched by your support," Lily said, "but no matter how supportive you are, it won't do us a bit of good if Sheila and Tracee go blabbing about us all over town."

"I wouldn't worry about Sheila and Tracee," Big Ben said. "I took care of them."

Lily thought of all those stuffed hunting trophies that littered the McGilly house. "You didn't . . . shoot them, did you?"

Big Ben let out a big belly laugh and slapped his thigh. "Naw, honey, I didn't shoot 'em. 'Course, I'd like the sight of my bank book a little better if I had shot 'em. I bought 'em off... it was the easiest thing in the world. You give 'em a little money to buy somethin' shiny with, and they'll shut right up. They're no better than magpies, those women. I went to the safe in the house and peeled 'em each off five thousand-dollar bills — pocket change was all it was. I told 'em if they breathed a word of what they seen at your house, that'd be the last of my money they'd ever see."

Ben shook his head in wonder, and Lily rose to kiss Big Ben and Jeanie. "You're the best father- and mother-in-law a lesbian in a sham marriage ever had."

The doorbell rang before Lily had a chance to sit down. She opened the door to see Granny McGilly, holding the sleeping Mimi in her arms.

"I took her to the playground over in Callahan and ran her some," Granny said. "Once the car started moving, she went out like a light."

Lily took Mimi from Granny McGilly and held her close. The little girl smelled of sunshine and sleep, and Lily inhaled deeply.

The courtroom of the Faulkner County Courthouse did not have the polished wood sheen of courtrooms on TV shows. The once-white walls were dingy, and Lily, Ben, and Buzz Dobson were seated at a cheap folding table. Ida, Charles, and Mike Maycomb, with their Italian-suited attorney, sat at a folding table opposite of them. With its dinginess and cheap furniture, the room looked like an approximation of a courtroom for a high school production of *Inherit the Wind*.

The entrance of Judge Sanders failed to fill Lily

with hope. Despite the fact that he was supposedly the official property of the McGilly family, the judge's dour expression did not inspire confidence. Stooped and scowling, he looked as ancient and stodgy as some of the living fossils on the U.S. Supreme Court.

Judge Sanders croaked at the Maycombs' attorney to make his opening remarks. Stephen J. Hamilton stood before the judge, wearing a suit that probably cost more than the sum total of all the clothing Lily had bought in her life. His artfully woven hair, his bronze skin — everything about him said big-shot, big-city lawyer. Lily hoped that Judge Sanders wasn't impressed by flashy appearances.

"Your honor," Hamilton began, "I am here to speak today about the value of a child. Those of us in this courtroom who are parents know the joy of holding a new baby for the first time, and any good parent will tell you that a child is more precious than diamonds, more valuable than gold." Lily watched the gold and diamond ring glint on his right hand. "The value of a happy child, a loved child, a child raised by strict but loving parents in a morally sound home, is immeasurable. These children are worth more than their weight in diamonds and gold. These children are our country's most valuable resource, for in, their tiny hands, is our future.

"But," Hamilton said, letting his tone grow somber. "What about the other children? Children raised in morally unfit homes? Children without a real mother and father to love them, to discipline them, to teach them right from wrong? What about these children's future? And how will these children affect our future? Will they grow up to be criminals, drug users, moral degenerates — all because of the lack of a suitable family environment?

"Today we are here to determine the future of one child. The child in question, Mimi Maycomb, is not yet two years old, still innocent, still reasonably untouched despite the circumstances into which she was born.

"Children don't ask to be born, after all. But some children are lucky. They are born to a mother and father who are married in the eyes of God and the state, a mother and father who have the spiritual, moral, and financial capability to properly care for them." He stopped to sip from a paper cup of water, then looked up with sorrowful eyes. "Other children are not so lucky. They are born into impoverished, single-parent homes. They are born to irresponsible parents who neglect or abuse them. Or they are born into homes that are so morally degenerate that they will never learn how to follow the correct moral and spiritual paths. This last breed of children suffers from the worst type of poverty of all — moral poverty. Mimi Maycomb is one of these morally impoverished children."

In her seat, Lily gripped the edge of the table as though it were the safety bar on a rapidly plummeting roller coaster. She looked at Buzz Dobson sitting there in his stained and rumpled seersucker suit, with a placid, bovine expression. It was all she could do to stop herself from biting her nails.

"Let me share with the court," Hamilton continued, "the story of Mimi Maycomb's birth." He smiled, revealing a mouthful of perfectly white, capped teeth. "The story's a little more complicated than the story of most births, so bear with me. Charles and Ida

Maycomb, the fine folks sitting over there at the petitioner's table, are the parents of the now-deceased Charlotte Maycomb. I have no idea why this happened, because I know Charles and Ida to be good parents . . . still, no matter how good a shepherd is, one of his sheep will stray. Charlotte Maycomb strayed from her parents' guidance and entered into a homosexual relationship with the respondent, Lily McGilly, née Fox."

Judge Sanders' scowl might have been the same one he had been wearing, but Lily felt it was now directed at her. Just as she was about to resort to nail biting, she felt the comforting hand of Jeanie McGilly on her shoulder. Once again, she was overcome by the depth of the McGillys' supportiveness. Big Ben had taken his first day off in the history of the Confederate Sock Mill to be with them at the hearing.

"Miss Maycomb and Miss Fox," Hamilton continued, "decided to do that which no two women can do naturally: They decided to have a child." Hamilton paused, Lily assumed, to let this scandalous bit of information sink in. "With the use of a sperm donation, they conceived the baby through completely artificial means. And so this was the home into which Mimi Maycomb was born, a home in which homosex-yoo-ality" — he stretched the word out, making it sound extra nasty — "was the norm. A home in which both parents wore the pants in the family, and both parents were women. A home in which books and films depicting homosexual acts could be found. A home where the only regular guests were other homosexuals. A home where no definition of normality could be found."

Hamilton took another sip of water, then continued, "When Charlotte Maycomb died in the spring of this year, she left a will that specified that custody of Mimi should be awarded to Lily Fox, her homosexual lover. My clients, Mr. and Mrs. Maycomb, are suing Lily McGilly, née Fox, for the custody of their granddaughter, Mimi Maycomb. They regret that their daughter strayed from their teachings and believe that by raising Mimi in a loving, Christian home, both they and Mimi can have a second chance."

He glanced at the table where Lily, Buzz, and Ben sat. "According to Georgia state law, the court may terminate custody if the child is deprived and if the deprivation the child suffers will likely result in physical, mental, moral, or emotional harm. Mimi Maycomb is not a physically deprived child. I have no doubt that, as Mr. Dobson will tell you, her basic physical needs are provided for. But what of her moral needs? What of the need to be raised in a morally fit home in which her guardians serve as good models for her future behavior? Just as a child deprived of food lacks proper physical nourishment, Mimi Maycomb lacks proper moral nourishment. She hungers for the court to do the right thing — to put her in a home where she herself can grow up to do the right thing and to be a decent, normal young lady.

"You'll hear a lot of things from the respondent today. Mr. Dobson is going to tell you that by marrying Mr. Benny Jack McGilly, Lily Fox showed a desire to raise Miss Maycomb's child in a normal, two-parent heterosexual home. He may also tell you that Mimi Maycomb is the biological child of Charlotte Maycomb and Benny Jack McGilly — a claim for which no medical proof has been offered. Through the testimony of Charlotte's family and through the use of a piece of videotaped evidence, I intend to show that whether they are married or not, Lily McGilly and her husband of convenience cannot provide a morally fit home for Charlotte Maycomb's daughter. The only home they can provide is one that lacks moral fiber and will ultimately harm young Mimi.

"If the value of a child is beyond that of gold and diamonds, we would be selling Mimi short by placing her in an environment that values sodomy over Sunday school. The future of a child is in your capable hands, Your Honor, and I pray that you make the right decision."

Lily's mind reeled. What was this "videotaped evidence" Hamilton had mentioned? Was it one of those loony antigay documentaries produced by the Christian right? Or — Lily shuddered — hadn't she and Charlotte videotaped themselves having sex once? But they had erased it after they'd watched it. Hadn't they? Lily was so busy panicking she didn't even hear the judge ask Buzz to make his opening remarks.

When she looked up, she saw Buzz standing before the judge in a suit that looked as if it had been slept in last night and then used as a napkin this morning.

"Your Honor," Buzz began, "I wanna tell you a little about my client, Lily McGilly. Mrs. McGilly is an award-winning author and illustrator of several books for children. In her hometown of Atlanta, she did a great deal of volunteer work for organizations that helped women and children. She has volunteered to teach art classes for after-school programs for under-privileged youth and has helped prepare food in soup kitchens that feed hungry children and their parents. Mrs. McGilly's love for children is so strong that when her friend Charlotte Maycomb made up her will, she knew that Mrs. McGilly would be the best person to care for her baby girl.

"And when Lily Fox married my other client, Mr. Benny Jack McGilly, whom we believe to be Mimi Maycomb's biological father, they entered into marriage in the spirit of creating a stable, loving family for Mimi to grow up in. Through the testimony of members of the McGilly family, I intend to show that Mr. and Mrs. Benny Jack McGilly have created a stable, loving family. Charlotte Maycomb's wishes should be respected."

"Is that all?" Judge Sanders asked.

"Yes, Your Honor, that'll do it," Buzz said, returning to his seat.

Lily had serious doubts that Buzz's opening remarks would "do it." Not only were they brief compared to Hamilton's, they lacked Hamilton's sense of theater. Also, while Hamilton's entire argument was built on the perceived evils of homosexuality, Buzz didn't even touch on the gay issue.

Lily looked at Ben, whose face was an unreadable mask. He might still be under the impression that the McGilly family name would get them out of this mess, but Lily thought differently. Things looked bad.

Hamilton's questioning of the Maycombs only made it worse. When Ida Maycomb took the stand, Hamilton spoke to her in soft, gentlemanly tones. "Mrs. Maycomb, I know this is a difficult subject for you, but I want you to recount for us a conversation your daughter had with you six years ago, after she had met Mrs. McGilly."

Ida Maycomb was the very image of the tragic, martyred mother. On some level, Lily was sure, she was enjoying her role in this drama. "She called me up one day and said there was something she had to tell me . . . and it had to be in person. So she invited me to lunch the next day. Of course, I was dying to know what it was she had to tell me. I thought to myself, maybe she's finally found a man who's agreed to marry her." She shook her head sadly. "But of course, that wasn't it."

Ida looked down and cleared her throat. "I went to her apartment for lunch. I remember she'd made a tuna salad that had too much celery seed in it. Charlotte never was much of a cook —"

"Mrs. Maycomb," Judge Sanders interrupted, "in the interest of our getting to have some lunch today, could you please stick to the topic at hand?"

"I'm sorry, your honor. It's just that it's so difficult . . ." She began to sniffle. Hamilton pulled a small packet of Kleenex from his jacket pocket. She took one and dabbed at her eyes. Lily wondered how many times they'd rehearsed that little exchange. "Continue when you're ready, Mrs. Maycomb," Hamilton said soothingly.

Ida took a deep breath and continued. "We sat down to lunch. Charlotte was just playing with her food, not really eating, and she said there was something she'd been meaning to tell me for a long time, but she had just kept putting it off. Now, she said, she couldn't put it off any longer. 'Mama,' she said to me, 'I'm . . . I'm a . . . lesbian.'" Ida said the word *lesbian* as though she was sounding it out from a dictionary's pronunciation key. She wiped away another tear.

"And why," Hamilton asked, "was it that your

daughter felt that after all this time she had to tell you about her homosexuality?"

Ida looked at him with wet eyes. "She said she had fallen in love . . . that was how she put it, just like it was a normal thing to do. She said she'd been seeing this woman, and they had decided to settle down and make a life together."

"And who was this woman?"

Ida nodded toward Lily. "That's her, right over there."

"Thank you, Mrs. Maycomb. I know this is difficult for you. I just have one more question. A little over three years after the conversation you just discussed, Charlotte told you she was pregnant — that she had been artificially inseminated and that she and Lily were going to raise a child together. What was your reaction when she told you this?"

"Well, naturally, it just broke my heart," Ida said. "When you've got two adults who are sinning together, there's not much you can do about it. You can pray for 'em, and you can try to bring 'em to the Lord, but they're adults, so they're gonna do what they wanna do. But to bring a child into that sinful environment . . . like I said, the thought of it just broke my heart. That's why we want to raise Mimi ourselves . . . there's some things a small child shouldn't be exposed to."

"Thank you, Mrs. Maycomb. No further questions."

Judge Sanders nodded toward the table where Lily was sitting. "Mr. Dobson?"

Buzz rose and smiled at Ida. "I won't take up much of your time, Mrs. Maycomb." He was polite to the point of deference. Lily had to give old Buzz some credit for this tactic — in a small Southern town, you weren't going to win any points by being mean to somebody's mama. "Could you tell us, please ma'am, what your daughter did for a living?"

Ida looked puzzled. "She taught at Atlanta State."

"Yes." Buzz glanced at his notes. "At the time of her death, she was a tenured associate professor of English, was she not?"

"Uh, I think so." Ida's hesitation didn't surprise Lily. Ida had never taken much of an interest in Charlotte's career. "But I don't see what that has to do with the case."

"Well, the way I see it, Charlotte's achievements have quite a bit to do with the case. If she became a tenured associate professor at such a young age, it must have meant her colleagues thought she did a good job. And she must have. Her teaching evaluations were high. She published numerous articles and co-authored one published book. It seems to me that Charlotte's career is somethin' a mother could really be proud of."

Ida was clearly baffled about where Buzz's line of argument was heading. "Well, Charlotte always was . . . book-smart."

"It sounds like she was. And the reason I'm bringing this up is because, by giving her tenure, by promoting her to the rank of associate professor, her colleagues were saying that Charlotte was of sound mind . . . that she knew what she was doing, that she was capable of making decisions. And if she was of sound mind to make decisions at work, it seems like she'd also be of sound mind to make up her own will . . . to decide who should get custody of her child in the event of her death. What do you think, Mrs. Maycomb? Was your daughter of sound mind?"

"Like I said." Ida squirmed in her seat. "Charlotte always was book-smart, but she didn't have a lick of common sense. And when she hooked up with that one" — she nodded at Lily — "any bit of common sense she had went out the window."

"You don't like Mrs. McGilly, do you, Mrs. Maycomb?"

"Objection," Hamilton interrupted. "Irrelevant."

"Your Honor," Buzz said, "if you'll bear with me, I'll show how Mrs. Maycomb's and Mrs. McGilly's relationship pertains to the case."

"Go ahead then, Mr. Dobson," Judge Sanders said wearily.

Buzz repeated the question.

"Why, I don't think that question's fair at all." Ida's blue eyes were flashing. Lily had never seen her so openly angry before. "How would you feel if some . . . some lesbian came and seduced your daughter into a life of sin? Why, you'd just as soon see her dead as —" Perhaps seeing the rays shooting from Stephen Hamilton's eyes, Ida clamped her mouth shut.

"You are a Christian, are you not, Mrs. Maycomb?"

"I most certainly am."

"Well, aren't Christians supposed to believe in forgiveness, in people's ability to change?"

"I don't know what you're getting at, Mr. Dobson."

"What I'm getting at is . . . look at Mrs. McGilly over there. She's a changed person. She's married a nice young man and is raising Mimi in a normal small town with more Christians in it than you can shake a stick at. Don't you believe she's changed, Mrs. Maycomb?"

Ida looked at Lily as though someone was holding something foul smelling under her nose. "No, I don't. Not that one. Her sin's still in there. She's just covered it up with makeup and a nice hairdo."

"Let you who are without sin cast the first stone," Buzz muttered.

"Objection," Hamilton said. "Mr. Dobson is a lawyer, not a minister."

Judge Sanders shrugged. "Sustained."

Buzz smiled sweetly at Ida. "Thank you for your time, Mrs. Maycomb. No further questions."

Lily couldn't help but be impressed by Buzz's line of questioning. Certainly he lacked Hamilton's slickness and drama, but he did a good job of establishing Charlotte as a rational person and Ida as an irrational one. Of course, Judge Sanders had looked bored throughout Buzz's presentation, so maybe he preferred a dramatic argument to a rational one.

On the stand for Hamilton, Mike Maycomb blubbered for his sister's soul. "When I think of my sister, being eternally consumed by the fires of hell, all I can do to comfort myself is to save my niece from that same fate."

"It's interesting," Buzz said in his cross-examination, "how you say the only thing that can save Mimi is to raise her in a Christian family, and yet the McGillys are a Christian family. Why, I see Jeanie McGilly and Big Ben's mama over at the Presbyterian church every Sunday. Doesn't that sound like a Christian family to you?"

"It's Mimi's nuclear family I'm concerned about," Mike said, pronouncing the word *nuclear* as *nu-kyu-ler*. Lily guessed they didn't spend much time on vocabulary at the Christian junior college he had attended. "I'm sure most of the McGillys mean well, but Lily and Ben . . . well, I believe our attorney has some evidence that'll prove once and for all that whatever their relationship is, it's not a Christian marriage."

"Oh, so what you're saying is that Mr. Hamilton is about to pull out the big guns?" Buzz laughed. "Okay, then. No further questions. Hamilton, let's see what you've got."

"Because Mr. Charles Maycomb finds today's matter too painful to discuss publicly, he has declined to take the stand and has asked instead that I screen this videotape, which I would like to do now, with permission of the court." He held the videotape aloft in his diamond-ringed hand.

Judge Sanders sighed. "How long is this gonna take, Mr. Hamilton? The country club stops serving lunch in thirty minutes."

"The running time on this tape is three minutes and twenty-two seconds, Your Honor."

"Proceed."

Hamilton popped the tape into the VCR. Lily watched as the Atlanta skyline appeared on the screen. The camera panned a long line of men and women carrying rainbow flags and placards. It was Atlanta's gay pride parade — Lily wasn't sure which year, but it was recent, judging from the clothing and hairstyles.

A convertible in which a gorgeous black drag queen sat, smiling and waving, drove out of the camera's range, and then another group of marchers came into view, carrying a banner reading LESBIAN,

GAY, AND BISEXUAL PARENTS. The camera zoomed in on four faces. One of them, Lily noted with horror, was her own.

There, onscreen, were Lily and Charlotte wearing matching T-shirts that read GAYBY BOOM. Marching alongside Charlotte and Lily was Ben, wearing a white polo shirt with a small, discreet pink triangle on the chest.

There was nothing discreet, however, about Ben's marching partner. Dez was decked out in a hot pink caftan and a rhinestone tiara. Though he was not in full drag makeup, Dez was wearing hot pink lipstick and a set of false eyelashes so large that they resembled a pair of tarantulas resting on his eyelids. He held the tiny baby Mimi, who was laughing and cooing, high above his head, while he shrieked at the top of his lungs, "We've come for your children! We've come for your children!"

As the screen went blank, the only sound in the courtroom was Big Ben's laughter. When Judge Sanders banged his gavel, Big Ben said, still laughing, "I'm sorry, Your Honor. I couldn't help it. That Dez may have had ruffles on his drawers, but he was funny as hell."

Judge Sanders removed his glasses and rubbed his eyes with the palms of his hands. "Well . . . on that note, let's break for lunch. Court will reconvene at two o'clock."

Lily sat at the table as if she had been turned to stone. When Ben turned to face her, she whispered, "Lost."

Chapter 20

In Buzz Dobson's dingy office, over cold sandwiches no one seemed to have much of an appetite for, Buzz, Lily, and Ben grimly discussed the morning's proceedings.

"I just don't understand how that bastard got hold of that tape," Lily said, pushing away her uneaten sandwich.

"Oh, he probably got it from Charlotte's crazy brother," Ben said. "That group he's president of has a whole collection of videos of gay marches — so they can use them to show the evils of homosexuality."

"Well, I guess it doesn't matter how Hamilton got it," Lily sighed. "All that matters is that he got it, and now we're screwed."

"Come on now, Mrs. McGilly," Buzz cajoled. "We've not even made our argument yet. The testimony of the McGillys holds a lot of water in this town."

Lily refused to be comforted. "Yeah, well, it's kinda hard to compete with a man in drag shrieking, 'We've come for your children!' Did you see Judge Sanders' face when he saw that? He turned positively *gray.*"

"Well, all we can do is get out there on the field and give it all we've got," Buzz said.

Great, Lily thought. Super-slick Stephen Hamilton has proven our entire marriage to be a fraud, and now our lawyer thinks he's back on the high school football team. Well, what do you expect from someone who graduated from a law school in a building that sits smack-dab between a Krystal and a Church's Fried Chicken?

Back at the hearing, Jeanie McGilly testified that Lily was as good a mother as she had ever seen — that she not only saw to Mimi's basic physical needs, but also spent a great deal of time reading to her and playing with her. When Stephen Hamilton rose to cross-examine Jeanie, Lily's stomach knotted in fear for her mother-in-law.

She needn't have worried. When talking to Buzz, Jeanie's demeanor had been warm and maternal, soft as the petals of a magnolia. But when she faced Hamilton, her entire presence changed until she could've been Joan Crawford playing a tough-as-nails businesswoman.

"Mrs. McGilly," Hamilton smiled. "I just have to ask you . . . when you saw the videotape, the one with

Miss Maycomb and your son and daughter-in-law and the man holding Mimi who was shouting, 'We've come for your children...' " He paused. "How did you feel when you saw that videotape, Mrs. McGilly?"

Jeanie smiled a little. "Well, I didn't laugh out loud the way my husband did, but I did think it was kinda funny. I mean ... you just had to know Dez. He didn't mean nothing by what he was saying; he was just joking, like always. Benny Jack used to bring him down here to visit sometimes. We all just loved Dez. I cried my eyes out when I heard about the accident."

Hamilton leaned toward her, going for maximum drama. "Did it ever occur to you that your son and Dr. Reed, or Dez, might have been ... more than just friends?"

Jeanie rolled her eyes dismissively. "Sure, it occurred to me. I ain't blind nor stupid. But the thing is, Mr. Hamilton, after your children grow up, you still love 'em, but you leave 'em alone. Once they're grown, you've done your job. They're adults, and they're gonna do what they wanna do."

"But what if that behavior is harmful?"

"Benny Jack and Dez wasn't hurting anybody that I could see."

"And what about Mrs. McGilly?"

Jeanie blinked. "What about her?"

"Is she hurting anybody?"

"If you're saying she's hurting Mimi by being ... or having been gay, she most certainly is not. She's devoted to that child. She and Benny Jack both are. I've been proud of my son, seeing him take on responsibilities like he has."

"Mrs. McGilly's history of homosexuality doesn't concern you?"

"She and Benny Jack seem to have a happy marriage. And even if Lily is a lesbian, I don't see how it's any of my bizness."

"Well," Hamilton said, sounding worried, "Mimi is a *female* child. Aren't you concerned with the dangers of sexual molestation?"

"Why, Mr. Hamilton, I've got half a mind to wash your mouth out with soap! I raised three boys. Do you think I messed with them just 'cause I like men?"

"Well, no, of course not —"

Jeanie stood up. "Mr. Hamilton, do you have any more questions for me? 'Cause I don't want to waste another minute of my life talking to somebody as nasty-minded as you."

For the first time today, Hamilton looked flustered. "Uh, no further questions."

Big Ben McGilly also held his own on the stand. When Hamilton asked him his personal feelings about homosexuality, he paused a moment, then said, "It takes all kindsa people to make a world, Mr. Hamilton. When I was in the army, I worked with black men, white men, Jewish men, straight men, and gay men . . . and I never had a bit of trouble with a one of 'em. Seemed to me that's how it oughta be, all different kindsa people working together for one cause."

"But what about homosexuals who choose to raise children?"

Big Ben shrugged. "Hell, at least they choose it . . . not like most people who lets their baser instincts get the best of them, and then just start spitting out young'uns by accident. I know your kind always wants to see kids brought up in a home where the mother and daddy's married to each other . . . and where they believe in God and the Bible." Big Ben looked off in the distance for a moment. "Well, I grew up in a home like that . . . for a while, anyway. My mother and daddy was married and went to church every Sunday. Trouble was, every Friday night Daddy went out and got drunk as a skunk, then come home and beat the hell outta Mama and me. She finally got a bellyful of his meanness and run him off with a shotgun."

Lily thought of the shotgun in the back window of Granny McGilly's pickup. She had had a feeling the old woman wouldn't hesitate to use it, with cause.

"After Mama run Daddy off," Big Ben continued, "we was even poorer than we'd been before. But every day of my life was happier than when Daddy had been in the house. So what I'm saying, Mr. Hamilton, is I started out in a family that looked the way you think families is supposed to look. But I was a whole lot happier when I ended up in one of them single-mother families your kind is always railing about."

"I don't see how that relates to my question, Mr. McGilly."

"All I'm saying is that your way ain't always the best way, Mr. Hamilton. Just 'cause somethin' looks good from the outside, that don't mean there ain't somethin' bad wrong on the inside. And you might not like the way homosexuals are on the outside, but that don't mean some of them ain't good people on the inside."

"This is, of course, just your opinion, Mr. McGilly?"

"Of course it's just my opinion! And everything you've said today is just your opinion. Everybody here's got an opinion — that's what we need a judge for!"

Lily and Ben were both subdued on the stand. They answered Buzz's gentle questions as rehearsed, and when the time for cross-examination came, they each followed Buzz's instructions: "No matter how much that sonuvabitch tries to provoke you, don't say anything but that you both love Mimi and that you plan to raise her in a healthy, supportive environment."

When all the testimony had been given, it was nearly four o'clock. Judge Sanders took off his glasses and rubbed his eyes. With his glasses back in place, he said, "We've heard some very persuasive evidence from both sides today," he began, "but it seems to me that there is one factor that has been overlooked — or intentionally ignored — by both Mr. Hamilton and Mr. Dobson, the claim that Mr. Benny Jack McGilly is Mimi Maycomb's biological father. If Mr. McGilly is indeed the child's father, it is only fitting that I give custody to Mr. McGilly, and, of course, his wife."

Judge Sanders sucked in his breath, then exhaled. "However, Mr. McGilly's claim to paternity is unproven. If Mr. McGilly is not the child's father, certain evidence — particularly the video evidence presented by Mr. Hamilton — persuades me that the Maycombs could provide Mimi Maycomb with a healthier, more morally sound home environment."

He took off his glasses to rub his eyes again. Lily wished his eyeballs would fall out into his hands. "Mr. Benny Jack McGilly," the judge intoned, "I order you to submit to a DNA test to determine paternity. If you are Mimi's father, in the interest of the rights of biological fathers, I will award custody to you and your wife, Lily McGilly. In the event that you have deceived this court and are not Mimi Maycomb's father, custody will be awarded to Mr. and Mrs. Charles Maycomb."

The judge looked at Ben. "Mr. McGilly, I've already talked to the folks at the lab over at Faulkner County Hospital. I explained the rather urgent nature of this case, and they said if you come in at eight A.M. tomorrow and bring Mimi, they can rush the blood samples down to Atlanta and have the results by Monday morning. Is that agreeable to you, Mr. McGilly?"

"Yes, sir." Ben's face was as white as a sheet of paper. Lily remembered what he had said when they were hatching this ill-fated scheme: "Nobody in Faulkner County is gonna make a McGilly submit to a DNA test."

"All right, then," Judge Sanders said. "Court will reconvene Monday at ten A.M., at which time the test results will be revealed and custody will be determined."

Jeanie hugged Lily, and Ben clapped his son on the back. "Looks like y'all are about outta the woods!" Big Ben said, grinning.

"I can't believe Jake Sanders would make a McGilly take a DNA test!" Ben was clearly incensed.

Lily, however, didn't have enough fight in her to be incensed. The judge's decision had made it official: She had lost everything.

"Well, now," Big Ben said to his son, "a judge is an elected official. If he came across like he was giving custody to a coupla homos without there being any scientific reason for it, he'd get voted outta office before he knew what hit him. This way, he can make it seem like the DNA test made the decision, not him. I know you don't wanna have to go through the rigmarole of getting tested, but after the results get back, you've got no worries."

"Right," Ben muttered. "No worries."

Chapter 21

It was awful, hearing Mimi wail as the lab technician pricked her to collect the blood sample. But it was even more awful knowing that this fleeting bit of pain was the least of Mimi's problems.

What kind of woman would Mimi grow up to be, being raised by the Maycombs? Would she rebel like her mother, by becoming a radical intellectual? Or would she rebel in a more reactionary and self-destructive way, by turning to drugs and promiscuous sex at an early age? Or, Lily worried, would she not rebel at all? Would she swallow every idea that the Maycombs spoon-fed her and grow up to be a self-righteous fundamentalist housewife who thanked the good Lord that Ida and Charles and Mike had saved her from being raised by a godless degenerate?

Lily, Ben, and Mimi crossed the hot asphalt of the hospital parking lot. "Well, I guess that's that," Ben said.

"That's all you can say?" Lily yelled, not caring who heard her. Her eyes flooded with tears as she strapped Mimi into her car seat. "You drag me to this fucking hellhole because you have a surefire plan for me to keep my daughter, and when it falls through, all you can say is, 'That's that'?

"I know . . . I'm sorry. I really did think it would work." Ben started the car. "I was thinking . . . you and Mimi could always leave the country. I could have you back to Atlanta and on the first flight to wherever you want to go on Friday afternoon."

Lily didn't bother to wipe the tears that were rolling down her cheeks. "I never quite pictured myself as a fugitive from justice. Of course, it's not justice that I'd be running from."

She tried to picture herself raising Mimi in some unspecified foreign country. Before her move to Versailles, she had never lived anywhere but Atlanta. "Where would we go?"

"Amsterdam's a great city. Nearly everyone there speaks English."

"God, five months ago, I was thinking my life was getting too routine and that maybe I should sign up for a yoga class or something. Now I'm getting ready to hop the next plane to Amsterdam. There's something to be said for being in a rut."

* * * * *

Jack had taken the afternoon off so she could spend it with Lily and Mimi. Now Mimi was wallowing around in the front yard with Lily the piglet and a couple of ill-bred hound pups while Lily the piglet's namesake and Jack sat on the porch. "Ben told me he'd help get Mimi and me out of the country, if that's what I want." Lily's voice sounded as cold and dead as she felt.

"Is that what you want?" Jack sat on the porch swing next to Lily, her arm around her shoulders.

"No, not really. Fleeing the country doesn't appeal to me, but . . ." Lily watched Mimi giggling beneath a pile of pigs and pups. "God, just look at her, Jack. I can't let those people raise her."

"You know," Jack said, stroking Lily's hair, "Daddy left me some money when he died . . . not a whole lot, but it'd be enough for you to live on awhile till you get your bearings . . . wherever it is you end up."

"I can't take your money."

"Sure you can. If my money can help you, take all you want. Money's never meant much to me anyhow."

Lily was overwhelmed by Jack's kindness. "You've already helped me. You've helped me keep a modicum of sanity in an insane situation. I don't think I would've stayed here if I hadn't met you."

Jack watched Mimi play in the yard for a minute, then turned to Lily. "I'll sure miss you."

"I'll miss you too." Lily burrowed her face in the collar of Jack's hay-smelling coveralls and let Jack hold her while she cried.

* * * * *

The test results would be revealed in court on Monday morning, and so the days before passed like the last days of a death-row inmate's life — miserable, nerve-wracking, and yet over too soon.

When Monday morning came, Lily, with red, bleary eyes and a dry mouth, assumed her position at the table with Buzz Dobson and Ben. Jeanie and Big Ben sat behind them, supposedly for moral support, but their presence only made Lily more anxious. So much of the McGillys' support, Lily thought, had come from their desire to protect Mimi, since Mimi was a McGilly, even if her last name did not reflect that fact. What would they do when they found out that Mimi had no McGilly blood whatsoever?

Hamilton and the Maycombs sat at their table, looking crisp and confident. If Lily had held Granny McGilly's shotgun in her hands, she would have blown them all away.

When Judge Sanders took his place at the bench, he said, "We have with us today, Doctor . . . Doctor . . ." The judge looked at the brown-skinned young man seated in the courtroom. Doctor or not, he couldn't have been much over thirty. "You're gonna have to help me again with that name, buddy."

The young doctor smiled patiently. "Anuj Mahatjan," he said.

"Yeah, that's it. The doctor here has the results of Benny Jack McGilly's DNA tests in a sealed envelope." Judge Sanders savored the phrase "sealed envelope." Clearly, this revelation was high drama compared to the humdrum cases that were usually heard in the Faulkner County Courthouse. "Doctor, you may take the stand, if you like, and open the envelope there."

Dr. Mahatjan carried a manila envelope to the

stand. Lily had never looked upon an inanimate object with the amount of fear she felt for that envelope. Dr. Mahatjan opened the envelope with painstaking slowness. He removed some papers from it and looked them over for a few excruciating moments before he spoke. "The test indicates that Mr. Benny Jack McGilly and Mimi Maycomb do share the same genetic material. Mr. McGilly is Mimi Maycomb's father."

"I'll be goddamned!" Mike Maycomb blasphemed, at the same time Lily had been thinking the exact same thing.

"Thank you, Doctor," Judge Sanders said. "I'll retire to my chambers to do the paperwork. Custody of Mimi Maycomb will be awarded jointly to Mr. and Mrs. Benny Jack McGilly."

Lily was being hugged by Jeanie and Big Ben before she could even process the information she had been given. "Congratulations, honey!" Jeanie squealed. "I told you everything was gonna be fine."

Big Ben chucked his stunned son on the shoulder. "I knew it, boy! I knew it!" Big Ben whooped. "A McGilly man don't have to do nothin' but look at a woman to get her pregnant."

"Apparently not," Ben mumbled.

"Come on," Jeanie said, taking Lily by the hand, "let's be good sports."

Jeanie led Lily to the table where the Maycombs were arguing bitterly with Stephen Hamilton. "Frankly," Lily heard Ida say to her husband, "I'd be a whole lot more sure of this if they'd let a white man do the DNA tests."

"Excuse us," Jeanie said. Charles, Ida, and Mike Maycomb turned to face her, looking shocked. "I just wanted to let y'all know that you can visit Mimi whenever you want to." Jeanie's smile was sweet and welcoming. "But if I ever hear you say one hateful word about my son or my daughter-in-law, you'll never see hide nor hair of your granddaughter again." Her smile was just as bright when she led Lily away from Charlotte's slack-jawed family.

Soon Lily and Ben were in the car, on their way to pick up Mimi — Mimi who was theirs officially, who could not be taken away from them. Lily's happiness was overshadowed by only one minor factor: She was completely baffled. "So," she said to Ben, "how did you rig it?"

Ben looked as if someone had just shaved forty points off his IQ. "Rig . . . what?"

"Rig the DNA test! Mimi has the DNA of two dead people. So how did you fake it?"

"I honestly don't know what happened. I mean, Dez was the sperm donor for you and Charlotte, right? The 'designated wanker,' he used to call himself." Ben laughed. "I remember once he said to me — you know how Dez talked — he said, 'Benjamin, my dear boy, when I was sixteen, I never thought I'd get tired of wanking off, but dear god, this sperm donor thing is putting welts on my weenie. Now I know why Portnoy complained.' "

Ben laughed, and Lily joined him. It felt so good to laugh now . . . now that she knew that Charlotte and Dez's biological child would be raised in a way that would have made them happy.

Ben interrupted his own laughter with a sudden, "Hmm."

"Hmm, what?" Lily said.

"I was just thinking about how exhausted Dez got with the whole sperm donor thing . . . God, that seems like so long ago, doesn't it, when you and Charlotte were trying to get pregnant?"

"It was a while ago, I guess . . . almost three years."

"Yeah. You know, I hate to admit it, but after y'all pulled Dez's name out of the hat, I didn't pay too much attention to all the baby-making attempts. That was back when I was so in love with Chris, even though our personalities totally clashed. I was so obsessed with him, though . . . oh . . . my . . . god!" Ben lost control of the car, swerved, then finally regained control, and pulled over to the side of the road.

"What?" Lily gasped. "Are you trying to get us killed now that this thing's finally over?"

"No. It's just . . . oh my god."

"Talk, boy. Talk."

"I just thought of something. There was this one week when Charlotte was just sure she was ovulating, and you were getting two sperm donations a day from Dez, one in the morning and one at night. The poor guy was just whipped — he said it was apparently no myth about women being sexually demanding. Anyway, I remember one night I had been out with Chris, and we had had a big fight at the restaurant. I was so mad I stopped at Blake's on the way home and had a couple of drinks, just to calm down. And of course, you know my alcohol tolerance. I was bombed by the time I got home.

"I found Dez upstairs in bed, glumly examining this empty artichoke jar he was supposed to ejaculate into. He had all these boy mags spread around him on the bed, but his face just looked desolate. 'Benjamin, my boy,' he said to me. 'I just can't do it. I've come inside this jar so many times, I feel like I ought to marry it.' Like I said, I was drunk, and he was exhausted, so I just grabbed the jar from him and said, 'Oh, hell, let me do it.' "

"So the jar of semen Dez brought over that night was —"

"Mine. I don't believe it, though. I just did it that one time, and Dez did it dozens and dozens —"

"It just takes one sperm, honey." Lily laughed and threw her arms around Ben, who, for the first time, hugged her back with equal force.

As Lily walked up the path to Granny McGilly's house, the old woman opened the screen door. Mimi stood in the doorway, wearing a sunshine-yellow gingham sundress, and her face lit up like sunshine as soon as she saw Lily. "Mama!" she squealed and ran barefoot down the path into Lily's open arms.

Big Ben and Jeanie had told Lily and Ben they could invite anybody they wanted to the big celebration barbecue, and they had taken the elder McGillys at their word. Ken was there, and he and Ben were pushing Mimi around the pool on the inflatable raft while she lounged like a tiny bikinied goddess. Jack was helping Ben's brother Wayne tend the grill, while Honey was helping Jeanie set out the potato salad and baked beans.

"There's no telling when we'll see our better halves again," Jeanie laughed, in reference to the fact that Big Ben had just taken Mick into the house to show her his hunting trophies.

At the redwood picnic table, Granny McGilly sat with Dale and Sue, drinking beer and laughing about times no one else at the party was old enough to remember.

Sheila and Tracee gave the party's queer guests a wide berth, but they kept their pink-glossed lips buttoned tight. Big Ben had made it clear that any rudeness on their parts would incur his wrath, and he didn't have to explain that his wrath carried with it dire financial consequences.

"You wanna come for a swim, Lily?" Ken hollered, as he and Ben were taking Mimi on another circuit of the pool.

"Not with that brand-new tattoo on her back, she don't," Honey answered for her. "She's gotta keep it dry twenty-four hours."

Earlier in the day, Lily had an appointment at Honey's tattoo shop. On Lily's left shoulder blade, Honey had engraved the image of a peacock. Its feathers swooped and flowed with the natural curve of her back. It was Lily's first color tattoo, and it was stunning — rich with emerald greens and bright blues.

The peacock, Lily knew, would remind her of her time in the Peacock Alley region of Georgia, a time that had made its mark on her. But Lily liked the image of the peacock for another reason, too — its pride. Now that she had won Mimi, Lily planned never to hide her true colors again.

"Actually," Jack said, joining Lily by the pool, "I was just about to ask you if you'd care to take a walk with me."

"Sure," Lily said. "Just don't forget and touch my shoulder. It's sore as hell."

Jack smiled. "I promise not to touch . . ." She leaned closer and whispered, "your shoulder, anyway."

Jack unlatched the gate, and they walked in the

field beyond the McGilly mansion and pool. "So," Jack said, "what now?"

"I . . . I thought we were going for a walk."

"You know what I'm talking about."

Lily shrugged. "Well, I guess I'll take those animal sketches and work on turning them into a book."

Jack's grin had an uneasiness behind it. "That's not really what I meant either."

Lily smiled. "Well . . . Ben and I have been talking. He's gonna put his condo on the market. He and Ken are gonna try to get a place halfway between here and Atlanta, so Ken can commute to work, but they'll be close to the city, too. He and I are just gonna go our separate ways without making it official. We've seen all we want of courtrooms lately, believe me."

Lily knew she still hadn't answered Jack's question. "And me, well, I'm not planning on selling off Charlotte's and my condo yet. I figure Mimi and I will go back to Atlanta, and I'll work on the book. But there was something I wanted to ask you."

"Uh-huh?" Jack's eyes glimmered with hope.

"About Mordecai. I know Big Ben and Jeanie don't want him back, and he doesn't strike me as a condo kinda dog, so I was wondering —"

"Sure, I'll take him." Jack's voice was tinged with disappointment. "There's always room for one more at the farm."

Lily stopped walking and took both of Jack's hands in her own. "The thing is, you know how Mordecai is about me. He's really gonna miss me." She let go of Jack's hands and draped her arms over Jack's shoulders. "So I guess I'll have to drive up to the farm and visit him really, really often."

Jack grinned. "Oh yeah?"

"Yeah." Lily grinned back. "I'd say I'd need to visit him every other weekend at least. And sometimes Mimi could spend time with her mamaw and papaw while I spend some time alone with . . . Mordecai. If that's okay with you, of course."

"I think I could handle that." Jack leaned down and met Lily for a kiss, resting her hands on the small of Lily's back. When they parted, Jack said, "I do have a question, though."

"What's that?"

"What if in a year or two, I — I mean, Mordecai — what if Mordecai decides that he wants to see you more often than just on the weekends? What if he decides that he wants to be with you every minute that he possibly can?"

Lily looked into the light blue eyes of this woman who was willing to give her not only love but time, who was willing to wait until Lily had healed enough to marry her life with another woman's. "Well," she said, "if he feels that way in a year or so, we may just have to make arrangements such that the two of us can spend more time together."

"All right!" Jack hugged Lily close, careful to avoid her new tattoo.

"Well," Jack said. "I reckon they'll be wondering what happened to us."

"Let's go then." Lily took Jack's hand and walked across the field toward the fence that enclosed the pool. She was ready to rejoin the party.

A few of the publications of
THE NAIAD PRESS, INC.
P.O. Box 10543   Tallahassee, Florida 32302
Phone (850) 539-5965
Toll-Free Order Number: 1-800-533-1973
Web Site: WWW.NAIADPRESS.COM
Mail orders welcome. Please include 15% postage.
Write or call for our free catalog which also features an
incredible selection of lesbian videos.

SIXTH SENSE by Kate Calloway. 224 pp. 6th Cassidy James
mystery.   ISBN 1-56280-228-3 $11.95

DAWN OF THE DANCE by Marianne K. Martin. 224 pp. A dance
with an old friend, nothing more . . . yeah!   ISBN 1-56280-229-1   11.95

WEDDING BELL BLUES by Julia Watts. 240 pp. Love, family,
and a recipe for success.   ISBN 1-56280-230-5   11.95

THOSE WHO WAIT by Peggy J. Herring. 160 pp. Two
sisters . . . in love with the same woman.   ISBN 1-56280-223-2   11.95

WHISPERS IN THE WIND by Frankie J. Jones. 192 pp. "If you
don't want this," she whispered, "all you have to say is 'stop.' "
                                                ISBN 1-56280-226-7   11.95

WHEN SOME BODY DISAPPEARS by Therese Szymanski.
192 pp. 3rd Brett Higgins mystery.   ISBN 1-56280-227-5   11.95

THE WAY LIFE SHOULD BE by Diana Braund. 240 pp. Which
one will teach her the true meaning of love?   ISBN 1-56280-221-6   11.95

UNTIL THE END by Kaye Davis. 256pp. 3rd Maris Middleton
mystery.   ISBN 1-56280-222-4   11.95

FIFTH WHEEL by Kate Calloway. 224 pp. 5th Cassidy James
mystery.   ISBN 1-56280-218-6   11.95

JUST YESTERDAY by Linda Hill. 176 pp. Reliving all the
passion of yesterday.   ISBN 1-56280-219-4   11.95

These are just a few of the many Naiad Press titles — we are the oldest and
largest lesbian/feminist publishing company in the world. We also offer an
enormous selection of lesbian video products. Please request a complete
catalog. We offer personal service; we encourage and welcome direct mail
orders from individuals who have limited access to bookstores carrying our
publications.